Coveted by CHAOS

CKMC Series, Book 3

Linny Lawless

*To Kaitlyn
Love Free
Ride Hardcore
Linny Lawless*

Coveted by CHAOS

Linny Lawless

Copyright 2018 by Linda Lawson

All rights reserved.

This book is a work of fiction. Some of the places named in the book are actual places found in Virginia. The names, characters, brands, and incidents are either the product of my imagination and used fictitiously. Any resemblance to actual persons, living or dead, events or establishments is solely coincidental.

This book contains mature content and is intended for adults 18+ only.

Cover Models: Armando and Taylor

Photographer: Reggie Deanching - http://www.rplusmphoto.com

Cover Design: Melissa Gill Designs - https://www.melissagilldesigns.com

Editor: Hanleigh Bradley

Personal Assistants: Hanleigh Bradley PA, and Primrose Passage

Coveted by CHAOS

Playlist

"I Am the Highway" by Audioslave

"Like a Stone" by Audioslave

"Auto Rock" by Mogwai

"Strict Machine" by Goldfrapp

"Shape of Things to Come" by Audioslave

"Bad Things" by Jace Everett

"Wicked Game" by Chris Isaak

"Pussy Liquor" by Rob Zombie

"Dragula" by Rob Zombie

"Porn Star Dancing" by My Darkest Days, featuring Zakk Wylde

"Pony" by Ginuwine

"Closer" by Nine Inch Nails

"Wicked Game" by Ursine Vulpine featuring Annaca

"Earned It" by The Weekend

"Tainted Love" by Marilyn Manson

"Crazy" by Aerosmith

Coveted by CHAOS

Linny Lawless

Gunner

The only family I have are my brothers. The ones I fought with in the war and the ones I ride beside in my club, the Chaos Kings MC. I keep everyone else in this fucked up world at a distance. It's better that way, isn't it? One night I stumble upon the most beautiful red-haired vixen to ever walk this earth. Never did I think that the Cheetah Club would have the cat just for me. She's enticing, captivating, and decadently delicious. The sultry movement of her body calms the ever-growing darkness and pain that surrounds me. I want to touch her, to breathe her in. But can I do that without letting her see the monster that I am?

Fiona

The King comes in to watch me dance at Cheetah. He's unapproachable, unreadable but still I sense his primal sexual energy. Almost as if he's a panther on the prowl. He matches this cat well, if you ask me. He isn't like the others. He sees what others don't. To him I'm not wicked or repulsive. I see him as well, I see the way he carries pain and darkness like an albatross around his neck. This Chaos King may want me to be afraid of him, but no one frightens me though, because I am as cursed as they come. And the only thing he does is draw me closer. All I want to do is know his name and know how sinful his lips feel against mine.

Prologue

I covered my head as I sat on my knees at his feet. He slapped a brown leather belt against his thigh. The scent of mildew coming from the cement floor. One light bulb with a pull string above my father, the only thing illuminating us. *"Idolatry... Witchcraft... revelings, and such like...."* Father's voice slurred, and he spat and bellowed, *"of which I tell you before, as I have also told you in the past! They which do such things shall not inherit the kingdom of God!"*

"Please Caleb! Please Stop! She's innocent!" Mother cried as she stood on the wooden steps leading down to the basement.

Father turned, extending his fist, grip on the belt toward her. "Shut your mouth, woman!" He turned back to me, slapping my hands away. He grabbed a handful of my hair, yanking my head back to look up at him, his eyes bloodshot. *"Sinful whore! Witch!"* He released me, pushing so hard that I fell back, landing on my elbows. My green skirt with white daisies rose up bearing my thighs. His eyes pivoted to them. I was frozen still, terrified.

Father had punished me so many times before. I was a woman now and I knew my punishments would be far worse and degrading. Father had caught me dancing along to a pop song on the clock radio on my bedside table. My eyes had been closed as I swayed my hips to the rhythm to the sexy beat. My hands pressed down along my hips and thighs.

"Dancing! It's sinful! Disgusting! You're damned, Fiona."

Would I be able to survive another night or day in that dark closet? I was past sobbing but couldn't speak. Hiccups were the only sounds coming from my trembling lips.

My hand shot up as he reached for me again. "Please Father! Don't hurt me!" It was useless to plead with him. He grabbed my wrist, dragging me across the cold cement floor toward the back of the dark basement. I heard mother crying at the steps as Father released me and opened the rickety wooden door of the closet.

"No Father! Please! I will repent! I will take any punishment! Just please don't lock me in there!" I screamed, my throat so dry I only heard my breath, and not my voice.

Father heaved me up under my armpits and launched me into the small four by four foot closet. I flew forward and landed on my knees, scraping them. *"But the men of Sodom were wicked and sinners before the Lord exceedingly!"* He slammed the wooden door shut, the sound of the padlock clicking.

Light from the basement lightbulb illuminated through the slits between the wood slats of the door. Then the light went out. Total darkness. I screamed, balling my hands into fists, slamming my palms against the wood. No use. No one could hear me locked up in that small closet. My dark prison. My hell. I started to tremble and began to hyperventilate. I felt that my heart would explode in my chest. And still, no one could hear me. After a long while I went quiet and still. I wrapped my arms around my bent knees, leaning against the cool cement wall. Exhaustion. I needed to close my eyes to sleep, but I couldn't.

I eventually dozed off. My eyes flew open to the sound of the padlock unclicking. I sat up from the wall, running my hands through my scalp and grabbing chunks of my own hair. Was it Father coming back to inflict more pain with his leather belt against my thighs and my backside? The warped wooden door swung open.

"Fiona, its me. Seth. Come out." It was a hushed whisper. I could not see my brother's face, only his silhouette from the basement light bulb behind him. "Father left. "

He held his hand out and I grabbed it, coming to my knees and crawling out of the dark hole. I flung myself onto him, clinging tight. "Seth! I thought I was going to die in there!"

He squeezed me back. "I'm sorry I couldn't come quicker, sis."

I pulled away from him. His brows were knotted together. I saw anger. And fear. "My brave brother… I must go back in. He will hurt you if he finds out!"

I turned to crawl back in, but Seth took hold of my arms. "No Fiona. Go to your room and lock your door. Mother knows I came down here to get you out. Father will still be drunk off his ass when he gets back. I'm big enough now. I think I can take him." Seth was only fourteen years old. He was just a child. He'd seen all the things Father did to me over the years, ever since he learned how to walk. I broke down in his arms. He was all I had. Mother loved us, but she feared Father more. I looked into his eyes, so full of rage.

Later that night as I sat on my bed, hugging my pillow, I listened to Father yell at Seth from behind my bedroom door. Seth was wrong that day. He was not able to take Father. He was beaten. And he was the one locked in that basement closet for two days for taking me out of it. Father commanded

Seth to repent for his own sins because he was as damned as I was.

"

Gunner

My temples pounded. I draped my forearm over my eyes to block the muted sunlight coming through the bedroom window. I had had way too many whiskey shots the night before at the Cheetah Club. And I was a complete dumb fuck to ride my Road King as trashed as I was. All I could remember was stripping everything off and landing face down in my bed. All because of the red haired exotic dancer, who called herself Cherri.

Cradled in the crook of my other arm was soft warm fur. I uncovered my eyes and peaked through one to see Gypsy. She was curled up beside me, purring as she slept.

"How did you get down here again? Did Sam let you in?" Gypsy opened her eyes and meowed. I sat up and groaned. My movement forced her to get up, arch her back and start her morning primping that cats usually do.

I had my good share of lap dances and spent plenty of money in exotic dance clubs. But there was something about Cherri. The way she moved seductively around the dance pole put me in some kind of calm trance, like popping a Xanax, giving me that warm relaxed feeling in the pit of my stomach. But not only did she give me those feelings of calmness, she made my dick hard as a rock.

The Chaos Kings brought Skully to Cheetah a few months back to celebrate his patch in with the club. That was the first time I saw Cherri. Skully had received more than his share of lap dances that night, so when Wez told me he was going to get the red haired siren to lap dance on him, I nodded my head toward a cute brunette dancer. "Not the redhead. Offer some bills to that brunette over there."

Wez had let out a little chuckle. "Ok brother. I get it."

Gypsy jumped off my bed and scampered up the stairs to find Sam. She was cooking breakfast up in the kitchen. I smelled the bacon, eggs and coffee. I scooted off the bed to put my jeans on that I had left rumpled on the floor by my boots. I climbed up the stairs to find Sam at the stove with a spatula in her hand. Ratchet sat in his spot at the kitchen table, drinking his coffee.

I found Gypsy again, sitting in my chair at the table. "Had enough of you already. Go." I shooed her off and planted my ass in it.

"Looks like you pounded a few down again last night." Ratchet could already tell.

I combed a hand through my messy bed hair. "Yeah."

"At the clubhouse?"

"Nah. Cheetah Club."

"Again?"

Sam handed me a cup of coffee, just the way I like it. "Thanks darlin." I took a sip and looked back at Ratchet. "Yeah. Again. Nothing going on last night at the clubhouse, so I wanted to watch Cherri again."

"Watch her, what? Dance? Or watch *over* her?"

Ratchet knew me all too well. "Both. I guess."

He shoved a fork full of Sam's scrambled eggs off his plate. "You haven't asked her for a private dance yet?'

"Nah. Just like watching her. She's a good dancer. This sounds fucking weird, but when I watch her, it calms me. I'll have a drink or two. Sometimes the other girls offer a dance or something private. But I don't go there for that."

Sam placed a hand on my forearm, her eyes soft. "Are you taking your meds, Gunner?"

I placed my hand over hers, giving her a crooked smile. She was a good woman. "Yeah darlin. Just like the doc tells me to." I knew she was concerned so I didn't tell her how those meds and the whiskey didn't mix well sometimes. Or how the throbbing painful headaches still came and went.

Ratchet swallowed down his first bite. "Hell, that girl has probably dealt with a bunch of fucked up ass-hole customers. So, you just being there to admire her might tweak her interest in you brother."

The only way I would be able to tweak her interest in me was to pay her for it.

Fiona

He came into the Cheetah Club again the night before. He never requested a private dance in one of the VIP rooms but sat at a small table in the corner of the club, just to watch me dance. He had dark brown hair, with a dark beard. Both his shoulders and arms were covered with tattoos. He was built but not huge or bulky. It was the way he walked that caught my attention; a confident posture, and with wide steps, like a panther stalking his prey. I knew he was a member of the motorcycle club, Chaos Kings. He came in with them over a month ago, celebrating with one of their new members who had just joined their club.

After their party, he would come in alone, always in the same spot at least once a week. I was aware of his presence, catching him in my peripheral vision as I danced on the front stage. I struggled to focus, dancing and smiling at the men who came up to slip money into my g-string while knowing that the Chaos King was sat at his table, drinking his whiskey and watching me dance. Only me.

This night was like any other night, and I was requested by a customer in the club who wanted a private dance in the VIP. He was a polite middle aged man, so I gave him a good private dance for thirty minutes. When I got back to the dressing room, I peeked through the side door that overlooked stage, just to get another look at the biker. He waited until I left the VIP before he paid his tab and left.

"That biker is smitten with you, Cherri." Destiny, the only dancer who would talk to me at the club, turned around in front of the wall mirror, wiggling her ass.

I watched the biker walk out the front doors of the club and turned to Destiny. "Yes. It seems like it."

"He's never slipped you any money or ask for you in the VIP?"

"No. He's done neither. He seems very comfortable with himself, but un-approachable." I began to dress in my comfy clothes, since that was my last dance on stage for the night.

"You just have that kind of effect on him babe. He'll come around one night. I bet he's loaded with money. And hung like a bull!"

"How have you come to that conclusion? That he's loaded with money, *and* well endowed?"

"You talk funny sometimes, Cherri. He's a biker. And he's in a bike gang. *That's* why I think he's loaded with money.

Do you mean a *big cock*? I'll bet he does! If you ever do get him in the VIP, will you find out for me? Please?"

I sighed. My skin was very fair, and it turned a faint shade of pink. "You have no filter, Destiny."

Destiny was a very sultry exotic woman. She was of mixed blood, half African, half Asian, with thick jet black hair that hung down past her shoulders. She was a stark contrast to me, with my Scottish blood, white skin, blue eyes and long red hair. It felt like a curse sometimes.

"It's not the colonial days, Cherri. You talk all prim and proper like you lived during the revolutionary war or something. But it's cute and sexy, I guess." she winked at me as I gathered my night bag and headed out.

I blew her a kiss. "Get rich tonight, darling."

She snatched my invisible kiss from the air and winked. "You know it baby."

Gunner

Another Friday night and the Chaos clubhouse was about to let loose. It was the beginning of Fall and the temps were getting lower and the leaves had started to turn their colors from green to red, brown and yellow. It was the perfect season for riding, just adding an extra layer of clothing. Chaos bikes were parked out on the lot, side by side. My brothers were all here, popping caps off beers to start the weekend.

I sat at the bar with Magnet as he waited for his two girlfriends to show up. I couldn't place their names, but they were hot and tended to Magnet's every need. The three of them were pretty care-free about having a good time.

Magnet shared a shot of whiskey with me. He slammed the shot glass on the bar. "You wanna team up with Brandy and Becky?"

I almost spat out my shot, but swallowed it down quick. "Team up? Man, that's all for you. I don't share when it comes to the females."

Magnet let out a booming laugh, shaking his head. "No brother. I didn't mean a *fuck-fest*. I meant teaming up to play a few games of pool."

"Well in that case, sure. I'm game. I'll set up the table." I climbed off the stool and headed toward the tables. "You wanna break the first game?"

"Yeah. The girls are pulling in now."

Being around laid back, pretty women was one of the good things about being a Chaos King. I admired the fairer sex. They came in all shapes and sizes, and they were all unique. I'd had my fair share of women, feeling their soft skin, and their luscious bodies. I respected them and liked to watch them from a distance. Like when they let down their walls and inhibitions, and just let loose to be free with their sexuality. Sometimes I'd get a pleasant view watching them dance topless on the pool tables at the clubhouse, touching each other. It was sexy. Of course, it got my dick hard sometimes too.

I teamed up with Brandy and we beat Magnet and Becky three out of three games of pool. Magnet wanted more punishment and kept his losing streak by getting Wez to play a game with him one on one. I left the clubhouse, strapped on my lid and started my Road King. Cherri was dancing at the Cheetah Club and I was headed there. The DJ at Cheetah, Jay-Jay, filled me in on her schedule.

I was there to watch her on a weekly ba͟͟͟͟͞w. Jay-Jay announced her as Cherri. When Cherri got on stage, my eyes locked with hers. There was nothing or no one else I could focus on for the rest of the night. Just her. She was gorgeous. Her long red hair fell to the curve of her heart shaped ass. I loved her creamy white skin under the pulsing disco lights. I knew other men watched her on stage too, of course. She was tall in her clear platform sandals. She moved her hips languidly along with a heavy beat of the music, thanks to Jay-Jay. I remember Chris Cornell's voice, as Cherri moved her hips, my eyes just roaming over her curvy thighs and calves.

But I left the club that night totally shit-faced. It started out good as I watched Cherri dance her two sets on the stage. Then some middle aged suit requested her for the VIP rooms. When he took her hand and followed her back, it took all I had to stop myself from following the man and jerk him off her. I didn't want his hands on her. But I inhaled deeply to get right in my head. I ordered an Irish Car Bomb. Then another. I didn't pay the tab and leave until I had made sure Cherri came out of that room, looking just as bewitching and beautiful as she had looked before she went in.

My dick had been already half hard as I pulled in and climbed off the bike in front of the Cheetah Club. Plenty of cars and trucks were parked near me as I heard the faint thumping sound of The Sopranos theme song. I entered the club and walked over to my usual little bar table in the corner and ordered a drink from one of the barely dressed waitresses. The dark haired beauty with the almond eyes danced on stage. Her moves were much more fast pumping and gyrating than Cherri's but just as alluring. She looked right at me from the stage and smiled.

Whistles and claps came from the men sitting around the stage as she ended her routine, shaking her upper body, making her nice tits jiggle. "Give Destiny some applause. Isn't she built like a brick house, fellas?" Jay Jay's voice came over the speakers. Destiny left the stage and the lights were turned down. "Now for our fiery red goddess... Here she is! Cherri!"

There she was. Her long red hair hung down in soft waves. A sheer tight green mini dress clung to every soft angle and curve of her body. It didn't hide her perky full tits, her nipples barely a shade pinker than her skin. She wore a black thong that showcased her plump and bodacious ass. She wore black high heeled platform stiletto heels. An Audioslave song vibrated through the speakers as she began to move her body. She danced around the silver pole with languid movement. My eyes roamed all over her. She turned and shimmied her hips, providing everyone a beautiful view of that ass! I just wanted to sink my teeth into it and spank it a few times.

The melody of the song turned to an easy guitar solo as she gripped the pole high, launching herself off her feet, flipping upside down, and spreading her long curvy legs into a split. I reached down under the table and pressed my palm on my stiff dick. The beast had a mind of its own. I sat still, my rational brain battling with that beast. I won. I calmed down. I downed my first glass of whiskey and the curvy waitress brought me another.

I had one of my blackout moments earlier that day. The hard pounding headaches, sweaty palms, and the anger rising like bile in my throat. I never knew what triggered it. It always came, and went. And came back again. But right then and there, all I was focused on was Cherri. She finished her first dance for the night. This time I wanted her in the VIP. Just us two. Alone.

Fiona

He sat at the same table as he always did. I walked toward him. He was slouched a little in the chair, his arms relaxed, one elbow on the little bar table, his hand cupped a half filled glass of straight whiskey, no ice. I stopped only two feet from him, flipped my hair back over my shoulder, tilted my head and smiled. "Hello handsome. I'm Cherri."

"I know. And I know that's not your real name."

My breath hitched at the sound of his deep voice.

"What's your name?"

"Call me Gunner." His voice arrogant too.

"Would you like to follow me to the VIP room? Somewhere more private?"

He stood up and offered his hand. "Lead the way, Cherri."

I reached out to take it. His skin was a shade darker, tanned, in contrast to my white skin. His palm was very warm. I sensed his eyes watching my ass as I led the way down the hall. I showed him into the room with the black velvet couch.

He sat into it, slouching again, his thighs spread so that I could stand in between them. Another Audioslave song began to play, through the speakers in the small dark room that smelled of sweet incense.

He watched as I swayed my hips slowly in a figure eight. I pulled my sheer dress up over my head, my breasts bounced just a little from my movement. I turned around and bent over, to give him a splendid view of my ass as I wiggled it. With my legs spread, I locked my knees, arched my back and flipped my long hair back over and stood up. I turned back around and climbed onto his lap straddling him. I began to grind slowly, back and forth against his lap, the only thing separating us was his zipper and my G-string. I could feel his hardness and girth.

He was huge. "You could hurt a girl like me with that…"

His large palms claimed my hips, preventing me from grinding on him. "Stop." His eyes met mine. "I wouldn't hurt you. I guarantee it."

His warm hand came up to touch my cheek. "What's your real name?"

His eyes, so dark, so intense. His hair, a little messy. The dark beard could not hide his strong angular jaw line. I could not deny him an answer. "Fiona."

His mouth was a straight line. He inhaled deeply. "Fiona. Say it again."

"Fiona…"

He groaned. "I like it." He closed his eyes and his head fell against the velvet couch. His hands kept a strong grip on my hips.

The moment of silence between us felt weird. "Don't you want me to dance for you?"

"No. Don't move. Just stay right there. Put your fingers on my temples." I reached up and placed my fingertips on his temples. "Rub. In circles. Do you like to sing?"

It was a very odd question for a customer who paid for a private lap dance. "Yes. Well. I cannot carry a tune though."

"You don't have to. Just hum for me."

I couldn't think of a song to hum at that moment. He had me frazzled. My pulse raced a bit just from sitting on his lap. He was still hard, and I didn't doubt it would stay that way. I began to hum a tune, and continued to rub his temples. "Is this all you want?"

He moaned. "Yes, Fiona. I like the sound of your voice. It calms me."

I had given private dances to bikers before. Some of them just wanted to have a good time and get a hard on. Some wanted more than just a dance. And some were dangerous. But they didn't have to be a biker to be a dangerous man.

"I like the color of your hair. A long time ago, red hair was a curse, or a gift." His deep voice rumbled.

"Yes. And it still can be both today."

He opened his eyes. "Don't know what it is about you. But I feel grounded when you're near me."

It was getting too intense between us then. He captivated me with that voice of his and the way he looked at me, like he wanted to see inside me. I climbed off his lap. "I should finish my dance for you. That's what you're paying for."

Gunner came off the couch. He stood so close to me that I had to look up. I smelled whiskey on his breath as he exhaled. "Just wanted to hear your voice and know what you smelled like. This time. Maybe next time you can give me a dance."

He pulled his wallet out, and pulled out several twenty dollar bills. "Put your dress on. I'll take you back."

I must have said something wrong. One moment he was calm then stand-offish and cocky the next. I snatched up my sheer dress off the couch, pulling it over my head and wiggling it down cover my ass. "That's it?"

"Yeah. That's it."

"Then, ask someone else to hum for you next time."

His hand fisted into my hair, pulling my head back. It hurt but felt good at the same time. "No. Only you Fiona. Understand?"

I inhaled sharply. "Yes."

I took the money from him. He took my hand and led me out of the room and back to his table. I stood with him as he threw more bills on his table, grabbed his glass and finished off the whiskey. "I'll be back next week." Then he walked past me, and out the front door of the Cheetah.

Gunner

I liked the sound of her name coming from her own lips. Fiona. The red haired witch. I had watched her on stage for far too long. I had wanted to touch her. And now that I had, I was even more captivated. But now I wanted her all to myself. I wanted her to belong to me. And I didn't want any man to touch her. The sound of her soft voice humming a non-melodic tune in my ear, her soft fingertips rubbing circles against my temples stopped the pounding headache. But my hard dick raged on. I wanted to bury myself all the way inside Fiona. And Claim her as mine.

I stripped and climbed into bed. I gripped my hard dick and began to stroke it. My hands glided from the purple head, down to the base, against my balls. I closed my eyes and remembered how good Fiona smelled. Her long red hair surrounded her pretty face, her nipples the same light shade of pink as her cupid doll lips. Pre-cum seeped from the head of my dick and dripped down into my palm as I stroked it faster. My breathing was shaky. My leg muscles tightened. My jaw clenched. Her voice. Her soft thighs, hips. I exploded and grunted as an arch of cum landed on my stomach. My dick jerked and spasmed in my closed grip.

There was a lull in calls for a tow service the next day. Me and Ratchet hung out in the main office waiting for those calls.

I was kicked back in a chair, legs up on a desk, my ankles crossed. A balled up wad of paper struck me in the back of the head. Ratchet.

I turned around, witnessing him in mid-throw of another balled up wad. "Earth to Gunner. Wake up brother. You hungover again?"

"No man. Didn't drink as much as I did the other week."

"You went to see your red haired siren again?"

"Yeah. And she took me back to the VIP this time around."

Ratchet threw the paper wad. That one bounced off my forehead. He leaned back in his chair, and placed his hands behind his head. "Do tell."

"She's even more gorgeous close up. Sweet voice. She's got this innocence about her. Which is wacked because she *is* an exotic dancer. But she doesn't quite fit that mold. That was my impression anyway."

"So, do you want to know her better? Or just fuck her?"

I remembered asking Ratchet the exact same question about Sam not too long ago. "Yeah of course I wanna fuck her. But she's not interested. I'm just one of her customers at the club." And I scared her already.

"That's why you should take her *out* of the club."

"Take her out? Like a date?"

"Sure. Why not? It's a no brainer you like her."

"Don't think she's into men like us, brother."

"Well, you'll never know unless you shift it into first. And make your move."

Ratchet didn't say much, but when he did it was important to him. Before the Army and my tour in Iraq, I was a young man. I came back a different man. I was still *me,* but I left some of myself there. And brought back jagged, and broken pieces instead. Fiona would've probably liked the young man I was before the war. Not the man I was now.

Fiona

"So? Was I right? Is he hung like a bull?" Destiny's eyes all fiery and wide, waited for my confirmation.

"Yes. Ok? He's huge." A shade of pink flushed my cheeks.

"Geez Cherri! You're blushing! You've rubbed up on plenty of crotches by now. What's up with that?"

It was because I was truly turned on by Gunner. My nipples hardened just remembering the feel of his huge hard on as I grinded on his lap. "He calls himself Gunner. But I don't believe that's his real name."

"Of course not. That's his road name, or club name. They're not outlaw. And that's a *good* thing."

"Outlaw?"

"Yeah. They don't do any illegal business or activities, like drugs, prostitution, guns, gangster shit, Cherri. The Chaos Kings MC are legit, with families and jobs. They're a tight nit group. Very loyal to their own."

"How do you know so much, Destiny?"

"I've been around it for a while, sweetie."

I appreciated Destiny for her no filter, straight at you attitude. She was not concerned about toning anything down. She gave it to you up front.

"I have a client in one of the VIPs." I raked fingers through my hair in front of the mirror, straightening out my black tight dress.

I was looking forward to it, so that I could focus on something else, anything else other than Gunner. After watching me for months, he finally had me alone. It was like touching a hot flame from a lit candle. He gave off this standoffish vibe. But when I placed my fingers to his temples and hummed as he had asked, he was like a tamed panther. His voice was rough and deep. His size did frighten me a bit. Many men did not know how to be gentle, even when they weren't as well-endowed as Gunner. Then it was like the candle blew out. That's all he wanted from me. Not a lap dance, or a hand job. Or even a kiss. I had wanted him to kiss me. Something I had done must have turned him off.

I went into Jay-Jay's DJ booth. "Client in the VIP?"

He was just announcing the next dancer, Vixen, to the stage. "Hey hon. He went ahead in Room one."

Vixen started her routine on stage, the goth and heavy sound of a Marilyn Manson song came through the speakers.

I walked down the dark hallway to Room one and entered. It was dark with a leopard print wing back chair against the drawn purple curtains. And he was sitting in it - Kyle.

I spun around to pull the door knob and run, but he was quicker and on me in two seconds, pressing his chest into my back. My chest slamming against the door. His arms came up to cage me in.

"I wanted to surprise you, Fiona. I succeeded," he hissed into my ear. His breath smelled of liquor.

His chest kept mine pinned against the door. I didn't move as a flush of anxiety snaked up my neck to my cheeks. All I could do was respond and reassure him. "Yes. You did Kyle. You're hurting me. "

The weight of him was gone. "I wouldn't hurt you! As long as keep that pretty mouth of yours shut."

I turned around to face him. Kyle was always dressed in a suit when he came to see me for a private dance. I knew his wife. They lived in a nice gated community, working his busy high tech white collar job. He liked to spend money at the Cheetah and requested me in the VIP every time.

He reached out and latched on to my wrist, pulling me to the cheetah print chair. As he sat, I landed on his lap. He grasped my chin with his finger and thumb and turned me to meet his eyes. "So, who's the biker?"

I was never really good at shielding my reactions, and Kyle knew it. "I don't know his name. He just likes to come in the watch us girls dance."

"He likes to watch *you* dance. Have you fucked him yet?"

"No! He just likes to watch."

"Come on now, Fiona. Don't lie to me."

I had to keep him calm. "I haven't Kyle. I swear."

"Ok then." He suddenly pulled me tight against his chest, wrapping his arms around me. "Your'e such a sweet girl… I don't blame the guy. You're intoxicating."

He released me and made me stand up in front of him. He patted his lap with both hands. "Show me how you danced for him."

I began to move my hips in a figure eight for him. I rose my arms up above my head and caressed them, bringing them back down to my sides. His eyes moved from my breasts to my belly. They became hooded and full of hunger. He was getting excited. He reached for me, pulling me back onto his lap, so that I had to straddle him.

"You going to finish what you start this time? Or are you going to do a half-ass job like you did before?" He blamed me for his own incompetence. He couldn't get an erection.

He squeezed his eyes shut. I hoped it would end soon and he would leave. He growled and pushed me off his lap. I stumbled back but steadied myself.

"Don't bother. You're just a tease anyway." Kyle rose off the chair, tucking his wrinkled white shirt back into the front of his suit pants. He pulled out a wad of rolled bills and tossed several one hundred dollar bills at me. They hit my stomach and scattered to the floor.

He walked past me and out the door of the VIP. I knelt down to pick the bills up and folded them nice and neat. I combed a hand through my hair to brush it back and away. Kyle had never physically hurt me. He often watched me at the club, and had even followed me home one night. I seemed to attract men who wanted what they saw of me on the outside, not wanting to know who I was on the inside. But I was ok with that. It was better than to be seen as a reject, or disgusting, or wicked.

The way that biker, Gunner had looked at me. Not like a piece of ass. Not like some odd freak. All he wanted from me was my voice. He didn't demand anything else of me as I sat on his lap. There was no way he could have hidden the enormous bulge in his jeans, right there between our bodies. And I told him my real name the moment he asked. That rattled me a bit too. I wasn't afraid of him. Only the size of him.

Destiny just ended her last dance on stage as I followed her back into the dressing room. The next dancer, Kesha, was fluffing her hair and adjusting her bikini in the mirror.

"Where do bikers go, Destiny?"

She was wiping sweat off the back of her neck with a towel. "Go? You mean where do they hang out?"

"Yes."

"Well *your* biker *does* hang, doesn't he?" She laughed.

"Destiny. Seriously. Where?"

"Why? You want to stalk him like Kyle, does you?"

"No." I blushed because Destiny could read me all too well. "I just want to know his real name. I know it's not Gunner."

"Just so you know hon, I don't think any of those Chaos Kings would like it too much if you started following one of them around."

"I will be discreet. Unnoticeable."

"You? Unnoticeable? Now that's funny *mon-cheri*" Destiny's French accent sultry.

"Please Destiny? Where do bikers like him hang out?"

She sighed and looked up at the ceiling before providing me answers, "I know of one biker bar called the Crow Bar. In town. There's a couple of other dive bars that I've heard of too."

I pulled my duffle bag out of one my locker and changed back into my clothes I wore when I came to work that day. "Thanks Destiny."

"Are you going there now?"

"Yes. I'm off now. Why not?"

Gunner

It took a couple of days, but the meds were finally kicking back into my system. I'd been off them for about a month but had gone to see the doc at the Fort Belvoir VA to prescribe me more. If anything, it helped with the flashbacks and waking up drenched in a cold sweat. It had also been two years now since Ryan's suicide. He was my brother, the main gun loader on the Abrams tank, deployed in Iraq. He had suffered from the demons of PTSD as much as I did, but then turned a gun on himself. I had been to visit his grave earlier that day, at the National Cemetery in Arlington.

And tonight, I had to get out alone. The Fall chill was setting in, but not too cold yet to ride the Road King down back roads close to home. The chilly wind pushing against me felt good. Made all that heavy weight whip off my shoulders. I ended up kicking my stand down in front of the Crow Bar. It was familiar, and close by, yet out of the way from everything and everyone around me.

Grease worked the bar with the cute blond, Lisa. She poured a Guinness in a frosty glass mug and winked when she handed it to me. "Thanks Lisa." I brought it up and took a nice long drink. The bitterness tasted good.

"Is it just you tonight, Gunner baby?" Lisa jutted out her hip, giving me a cute smile.

"Yeah. Just me." I winked back at her. "Maybe shoot a few games by myself". I headed toward the back of the bar to the pool tables.

"Well, if you get bored playing with yourself, come back over and shoot the shit with me." I thought about taking her up on that offer, but there were enough people at the bar to keep her and Grease busy that night. And I wasn't really in the mood to talk to anyone anyway.

After my second refill of Guinness, I aimed the cue ball behind the black number eight. I pulled back the pool stick. Red hair came into my peripheral vision from the front door and my aim was off as I took the shot. The cue ball smacked into the eight and rolled steady toward the corner pocket. And dropped in. I scratched. I never scratched.

I rose up and her eyes met mine. Fiona. My first thought – what the fuck was she doing here? I was used to seeing her gorgeous body, her breasts, her hips, and her long toned and curvy legs. But now she was in tight jeans, a dark green t-shirt that clung tight, and sneakers. My dick got rock hard instantly.

She didn't smile at me, and walked to the bar, planting that nice ass on a bar stool. Right next to her sat a couple of middle-aged men, weekend riders in their shiny new leather Harley jackets. And one of them I knew as Ted.

I guzzled the rest of what was left in the mug, pressing my palm against my crotch, and headed over to Fiona.

I heard the last thing that came out of Biker Ted's mouth. "Don't you dance over there at the Cheetah club?"

She nodded and replied with a smile, "yes, I do."

"I thought so. I bet you do more than dance, don't you? You are a sweet piece of ass…"

I slapped Ted across the back of his head. "Don't talk to her that way, dumb-ass."

He swung around on his stool. "What the fuck man? "

I was not in the mood to get my knuckles scraped by smashing it against his nose. "She didn't come in here to listen to *shit* pour out your mouth. Get up and move."

He climbed off the stool, throwing some cash on the bar. "I was done with my last drink anyway." And left. I planted myself on that stool, sliding my empty mug toward Lisa. She poured me another.

"I get that a lot. It really is not a big deal." Fiona's voice alto. Soft.

I turned to look right into her pretty blue eyes. "What are you doing here?"

"It's a public place."

"Yes. It is. What are you doing here?"

Her smiled faded. "I want to know your real name. I know it's not Gunner." Lisa placed a cocktail glass in front of her.

"It's Ethan." I brought the mug up for a drink, looking away.

I heard her pretty lips sip on the two little cocktail straws in her glass. "That's a nice name."

I shifted on my stool and turned back to her. She smelled like sweet honeysuckles. I was still hard. She looked down and noticed too. "Not a good idea. Coming in here alone. Just to find out my real name?"

She looked up from my crotch, her pink lips straight. She brought the straws to her lips again and took several long swallows to finish what was in the glass. Placing it back on the bar, she fumbled through her purse to find her wallet. "Sorry I ruined your night. I'll not bother you anymore."

She tossed a bill on the bar and climbed off the stool. I reached and grabbed a hold of her arm. "You don't bother me, Fiona. But I don't like to be followed."

"But it's ok for you to follow me? You watch me at the club. You finally had me alone in the VIP and all you wanted was for me to hum to you?"

I pulled her to my chest. She was so fucking soft. "I want more than that. Much more."

She exhaled. Her breath smelled like rum. "I'm not afraid of you. You can't scare me away."

"No? Well you should be." I didn't care if anyone was looking. I tugged at the collar of her t-shirt, leaned down and clamped my lips and teeth onto the soft juncture between her neck and shoulder. She gasped. I sucked on her flesh, then released it with a smack. A hickey appeared, the size of a silver dollar against her creamy white skin.

I looked back into her eyes. They were glossier, and hungry. "That doesn't scare me either. Show me more." She was a brave girl.

I released her and pulled away. I lifted the mug to my mouth again. "Go home, Cherri." I wasn't going to show her anything. She turned away and rushed out of the Crow Bar.

Fiona

I got in my car, shut the door, and turned the ignition on. But before I put the car in drive, I reached up and pressed my fingertips to the part of my neck that he just claimed. I got what I came to the Crow Bar for. His name. Ethan. The wall he built around himself was high. But I also felt his intense sexual energy. His eyes saying, he wanted to devour me. Right there in the bar. When his lips and teeth latched onto my neck, I lost my breath. I lost all reason. My heart pounded, and I shivered as the goosebumps along my arms rose.

And then as quick as two heartbeats, he released me. Pushed me away. The wall was back up. I didn't know anything about Ethan. Only that he rode a motorcycle and was part of the Chaos Kings motorcycle club. He did not frighten me though. Quite the opposite. He was intriguing, mysterious and crazy gorgeous. I wanted his lips to devour mine. I wanted to know what his tongue tasted like.

The painful feelings of being pushed away made me think about the home I left. My father. The shame. The fear. Of feeling worthless and disgusting. I was evil in their eyes. A whore. A temptress. I liked to dance. I liked to sing. I liked to touch my own body. But it was bad. Sinful. Strangers looked at me like that too sometimes. But not Ethan. He looked at me with adoration and desire. But not like a wicked thing.

I drove back home to my little one bedroom duplex. I was able to afford a living on my own with the money I made at the Cheetah Club. I rented from Libby, a nice elderly widow. She told me once that I reminded her of her granddaughter who lived in California. If I wasn't dancing, I was home. Everything for my modest home was bought used or from a local thrift shop. I decorated as best I could in bright, pastel colors. I had a couch, dinette table and a bed. That was all I need and made due with what I had.

When I parked along the curb in front of my house, I was only a few yards from the front door and noticed photographs taped all over it. I looked down the road and turned to look behind my car. There was no one around. The neighborhood was quiet. As I left my car and walked closer, I could make out the images taped all over the door. Naked bodies. Naked women, full exposure of their femininity. Still shots of porn from the internet. Women's faces close up with men's erections in their mouths. I stopped breathing. I spun around to see no one there. I turned back to the paper porn and ripped them off the door as fast as I could. I knelt, gathered them up and crushed them into balled up wads. I unlocked my door and threw them in the kitchen wastebasket.

I pulled out my cell phone and called the only friend I had. Destiny.

She answered on the second ring. "Hi Destiny. I'm a little shook up."

"What's wrong Fiona? Are you ok?" I could hear the thumping of the music from the club in the background. Destiny called me my real name when we weren't together at the Cheetah.

"I'm ok. Some one taped a bunch of pornography all over my front door."

"I bet it was that prick-asshole Kyle! Just be careful Fiona. You need to call Five-O. Now!"

"No. I tore it all down. I'm ok. I'm looking out the front window now. I don't see anyone or any cars that I recognize. I don't know how long those pictures were there today. I was out for a few hours. I just hope no one saw them, especially my landlord Libby! It would have really upset her!"

"I'm getting ready to get on stage. When I'm done, I'll clock out and come over ok?"

I didn't want to be alone. "Ok. Take your time. I'm ok... And thank you."

"Of course, mon cherri... "

Destiny was at my house within the hour. I showed her the crumpled up porn in my trash. She huffed, "it was Kyle. I'm sure of it. That mother fucker needs to be taken down a notch or two Fiona..."

"He's a nuisance, yes. But he's harmless."

"How do you know that?" Her eyes fiery, "You should stay with me for a while."

"I'll be ok. Really. He'll cool down. I'm sure of it."

"Well I'll stay with you tonight then."

And she did. I poured both of us some wine and we sat together on my couch sharing a soft fuzzy blanket. We stayed up and watched a romantic comedy movie together to help us both laugh and giggle.

The ending credits of the movie began. "I went to the Crow Bar and found him Destiny."

"Found who?" She took a sip of her wine.

"That Chaos King? The one that calls himself Gunner?"

Her eyebrows lifted as swallowed, "Yeah? Do tell! Give me the deets!"

"His real name is Ethan. "

"Yeah? And? Did you talk? Did you fuck him?"

My face turned a shade of pink to match the chardonnay in my glass "No! I did not fuck him! And he wasn't too happy that I was there. I know he's attracted to me. But he puts this wall up."

"Well I did warn you I didn't think he'd like you following him around like that."

"I know you did. But I can sense something in him. He doesn't look at me like I'm a piece of meat, or something disgusting."

"We're in the business of making money off our assets. So yeah, we may be just a piece of meat to some men, but we take their money and make a living off it too. And I really don't give a fuck what they think, or any of those other caddy bitches at the Cheetah."

"It doesn't matter anyway. I pissed him off." My heart sank again as I admitted it out loud to Destiny. And to myself.

Gunner

Even though it was the Fall season, Mother Nature wasn't yet ready to let go of Summer. It was a balmy ninety degrees on a Saturday afternoon. Not as hot as the Iraqi desert, but hot non the less. I worked the morning shift taking service calls for tows. Clocking out, I headed over to the Cheetah in my Ford truck. Cherry red, like the Road King. It took me a few days to swallow down my own pathetic guilt over what I had done to Fiona at the Crow Bar. I was a total shit for what I did to her. But DAMN! Did she taste like heaven when my mouth clamped down on her neck. It took all the self control I had not to scoop her up, plant her plump ass on that bar, yank her jeans off, ram my hard cock deep inside her and fuck her right in front of everyone.

And she just enticed me more when I looked into her pretty blue eyes. Brave. Aroused. She wanted more. Oh, how I wanted to give it to her too. But if I did, she'd see the monster.

A few cars and trucks were parked as I pulled into the parking lot. I headed toward the front steps, but the faint sound of a dog's bark steered my attention to a silver BMW. I saw the outline of the dog's head and ears in the driver seat. The windows were rolled up. I cupped my hand over my brow to peer though the window. A grey pit bull looked back at me, panting and whining. Its paw came up to the door panel. The car wasn't running. It must have been at least a hundred and thirty degrees in that fucking car. My temples suddenly began to pound and throb with blinding pain.

I hurried back to my truck, reached under my seat, and pulled out a crow bar that I kept hidden there. I raced back to the BMW and swung the crow bar, smashing the window. It splintered. The second swing smashed it; the glass exploded into pieces. I reached in and opened the door. The dog jumped out, panting and heaving. He was definitely male, his balls still intact. He sauntered back toward me and sat down on his haunches.

I dropped the crow bar and extended my hand out toward his muzzle. He sniffed me as I knelt down and took a hold of his collar. Black leather with silver studs. No tag. I rubbed his jowls as he drooled. I picked up the crow bar and the dog followed me as I headed back to the truck. He jumped right up into it as I opened the door and bounded over to the passenger seat. I started the truck and turned the A/C on full blast.

"Get cool, Trooper. I'll get some water." I shut the door and marched into the club.

Hank, the humongous bouncer, stood by the DJ booth, wearing a black t-shirt with white letters across his back, "STAFF". His arms were crossed over the tight fitted shirt. Half a dozen middle aged men dressed in plaid shorts colorful shirts looking like they plaid a round of golf, sat near the stage, drinking beers and watching the one of the dancers spin around the pole.

I approached Hank and cupped my hand up to him. "Hank, who drives the black BMW outside? Is he a regular?" I barked above the loud pounding music.

"That's Kyle's car"

My eyes scanned through the smoke, strobe lights and shadows of the bar. "Where is he?"

"He's in the VIP. With Cherri. Why Gunner? What's up - "

I sped past him, down the dark hallway to the VIP rooms. He came out of the second VIP room. Suit, loose tie. Kyle.

Fiona appeared right behind him. "Kyle, you can't keep doing this – "

He spun around, his hand enclosed around her throat, pushing her back against the door. "Fucking Whore!"

Throbbing pain gripped both sides of my skull like a vice. Suddenly it was tunnel vision, and all I could see was Kyle. Like looking through my tank's main sites, at the hashmark crosshairs. He was the target. It was an automatic reflex as I reached behind me for the revolver, pulling it out of the belted holster underneath my shirt. Grabbing his shoulder from behind, and slamming his back against the wall, I shoved the end of the gun barrel in his mouth. His widened fear as his lips clamped down around it.

I fisted my other hand onto the front of his suit jacket. My eyes bore into his. My jaw clenched and my teeth grinded so hard it intensified the pain in my skull. I shook my head back and forth. Slowly. All he could do was moan with the barrel shoved between his fucking yap.

"No! Please Ethan. Don't!" Fiona's cry halted my finger on the trigger.

"Fucks like you don't deserve to breathe." I yanked him away from the wall and shoved him hard. He stumbled falling backwards and landed on his ass. I stepped up to him, he scooted back on his hands, then gained his footing and ran.

I turned back to Fiona. Her hand was clutched to her throat, her eyes wide with fear. I put my revolver away, and stepped to her, cupping her soft cheek. "Are you ok?" She nodded, but her eyes began to well up with tears.

Hank appeared from around the corner. "Everything ok back here?"

I turned to look at him. "Yeah. Don't let that asshole back in the club Hank." Fiona pressed herself into my chest and started to cry. Hank left us alone. I wrapped my arms around her.

She was shaking. "He's never done that before," she mumbled against my chest.

I breathed in her familiar scent of honeysuckles, savoring it. "And he's never going to do it again." I tilted her chin up to look into her eyes. "Go tell Hank your taking the rest of the day off. I'll follow you back to your place." Then I smirked. "I want you to meet a new friend of mine. He's out in my truck."

I got one of the bartenders to fill a beer mug full of water and went back out to my truck to check on the dog while Fiona got her things. I saw through my window, that he seemed to be less in distress as he had been when I found him locked up in that asshole's car. The nice dry frigid air hit me as I opened the door and offered the mug of water to him. His long tongue lapped and gulped half of it down quick.

"Well who is *this* handsome fellow?" Fiona's voice came from behind me.

I turned around to see her dressed, with a backpack slung over her shoulder. Her face was even more beautiful in the sunlight. "That dip-shit Kyle had him locked up in a shiny BMW. He was close to being dead."

She came around me and offered her hand to him for a smell. Lucky dog. He licked her fingers. "I saw the broken glass over there… You saved him? He's beautiful. What are you going to do with him?"

"Not sure." I just stared at her profile. Her fair skin. Her high rosy cheek. "He can hang with me until I figure out something. Not sure how Gypsy will take it."

"Who's Gypsy?"

"She's one of my roommates." Fiona's eyes met mine. "She's a cat. She lives with me and my Chaos brother, Ratchet and his ole lady, Sam."

The side of her mouth lifted "Oh. Well. I'm sure this handsome fellow will be on his best behavior."

I had to look away from her blue eyes, "Which is your car? I'll follow you home."

I followed her white Mazda a few miles back to her place. The pounding throb in my temples subsided a little as I drove. The dog sat in the passenger seat, looking out the window, his long tongue hanging out the side of his mouth. I pulled up along the curb and parked behind her, in front of a row of duplex houses.

I reached over and scratched the dog's neck. "Not sure what your name is." I kept scratching. He barked. "So I'll just call you Trooper for now." I got out of the truck and he jumped out from my side, after me. He followed right along, as I walked beside Fiona to her house.

She unlocked and opened the door. "You are more than welcome to come in. Along with-" She looked down. He had slobber running down one side of his mouth.

"We'll just call him Trooper for now." I followed her in, Trooper right behind me. It was a nice little place, decorated in feminine light colors and flowery patterns.

She tossed the backpack on her couch and went into the little kitchen. "Would you like something to drink?"

I made my way to her couch and sat. Trooper was there on his haunches next to my knee. "Sure. A beer if you got any."

She came and sat next to me with two bottles and offered me one. "Thanks." I gulped half of it down. I was thirsty. And it tasted good. I placed it on her coffee table.

She lifted her beer to her lips and leaned back, I watched her throat as she took a good long drink. The throat I wanted to suck and bite on again. But her creamy white skin was marked with faint pink prints where Kyle had grabbed.

"So, who the fuck is Kyle? I don't want him anywhere near you. Ever again."

She placed her bottle next to mine. Combing a hand through her tussled red locks, she focused on Trooper. "He's a distant cousin. Him and his wife, Maggie, helped me when I left home and needed a place to stay. When I left my parents. And my brother. I came home after I saw you at the Crow Bar and found pornographic photos torn from a magazine, covering my entire front door. I knew it could only be Kyle who had done it."

I reached out and caressed the side of her neck. "He's dangerous."

"He's never done that to me before. He always looked at me the same way my father did. But this time he was angry with me."

I continued to stroke her pretty neck my fingertips. Her eyes were half closed. Her lips parted. "Look at you in what way, Fiona?"

"Like I'm wicked. Like I'm a disgusting thing. Like a whore who cannot be redeemed."

"You're NOT any of those things. You're beautiful. Breathtaking." I leaned in closer. And lightly grazed my lips against hers. They were so soft against mine. My tongue plunged through her parted lips and encircled hers. So delicious. I latched on and sucked gently.

I placed her soft little hand right on the top of my crotch. My dick was furiously hard and thumped against my zipper. She gasped. But I didn't frighten her, because she pressed her palm down and rubbed down the length of me.

"Hurt me with it," she whispered against mouth.

"No. I would never hurt you. Only gentle." My fingers moved from her neck to her collar bone, down to draw a circle around her budded nipple that poked through her tank top. I dipped down and darted my tongue around it. Her fingers snaked up the back of my skull and combed through my hair. My lips came over her covered nipple and sucked. Her back arched up to me, making my mouth clamp down and suck harder. She cried out and reached down with both hands, fumbling to unbutton and unzip my jeans. I wouldn't be able to keep that promise about being gentle at that moment. I released her puckered nipple and covered my hands over hers. "But not today."

Just then Trooper whined, his tail wagging. I grabbed the bottle and finished the rest of it and stood from the couch. My crotch was at eye level to Fiona. We both couldn't ignore my massive erection. "Gonna go now. Keep everything locked. Your door. Your windows. And Let me know if you see Kyle." I didn't give Fiona any time to reply, because I headed toward her door. Trooper whined again but stayed. "Yeah. Stay with Fiona for few days, Trooper." When I looked at her, I could see sadness in her eyes. "I'll go out and get him some dog food. I'll be back in a bit."

I got in my truck and drove to the local pet store. The pain in my head disappeared. But then my dick throbbed. Fuck! I was consumed by Fiona. And when Kyle's hand was on her throat, everything had gone black around me, like looking down the dark barrel of a gun, or through the optical scope on Lucy, the name of Abrams tank in my platoon. Rage.

I've killed men. Many of them. In War. If anyone tried to harm Fiona I would kill them too. I wanted to protect her. Watch over her. Fuck her. Feel her from inside.

Within the hour, I walked back into her house with a thirty pound bag of dog food over my shoulder, dog bowls and a few toys for Trooper. I gave her door three knocks. "It's Ethan."

Fiona opened it and went back to sit on her couch. I found the recipient of all these things that I just bought, snuggled up next to her. Lucky dog. "I wasn't gone for even thirty minutes and he's already made himself at home," I grumbled as I placed everything on her dinette table.

She petted top of Trooper's head, smiling. "Yes. Trooper is quite the guardian. And a cuddle bug too."

I came around to the couch and couldn't help but smile. He seemed well behaved. Fiona's eyes steered right to my crotch. Then looked up at me then. I took a deep breath in and exhaled to calm down the urge to pull out my dick and rub the head across her soft parted lips. I stepped back. And gave this my best shot. "Have you ever ridden on a bike?"

She blinked a few times. "No. Motorcycles seem dangerous but exhilarating too. I have always wondered what it would feel like though."

"It's Fall now, and the temps will cool down quick. But I think we should have a few more good weeks of riding. How about I take you out for one?"

Her eyes lit up and she beamed that beautiful smile. "Yes! I would like that very much Ethan. What should I wear?"

"Dress warm. Jeans. You have a pair of boots? No heels. A leather jacket? Shades?"

"Yes, I have all those things."

"OK then. I have an extra helmet that will fit your pretty little head." I smiled back at her. "How about Saturday morning? You off?

"Yes. But I will be working that evening."

"I'll pick you up at ten am then." I bent down and kissed her. And when I left her place, I counted every minute until it was ten am, Saturday morning.

Fiona

My fair skin always showed every blemish, but luckily, the red imprints from Kyle on my neck disappeared overnight. I let Trooper sleep on my bed that night. He curled up down by my feet, and I felt safe having a new companion. I always loved dogs but could never have a pet growing up in my household. Father wouldn't allow it. He saw dogs as just mangy scoundrels, that they liked to hunt in packs and follow the scent of blood. But I didn't see Trooper to be a dangerous man-eating terror. He had blue eyes, like me, that shown bright in contrast to his grey colored fur.

Hank the Hulk, as we called him, our bouncer at the Cheetah was such a darling. He let Tony, the owner and manager know what happened and reassured me that Kyle would never step foot into the club again. Hank was very protective over all us dancers and bartenders.

Hank was a giant of a man, bald, with a salt and pepper goat-T beard, and had arms the size of pythons. His size was intimidating and that's why he was there at the Cheetah. But only saw kindness in his eyes. Like a gentle giant. "Good thing Gunner was there for you, doll. That noodle dick probably pissed in his nice suit." His head fell back, and he laughed at his own words.

I blushed. How did Hank know Kyle had problems with getting an erection? I placed my hand on his huge bicep. "Well. Thank you, Hank. For letting Larry know and watching over me and the other girls here."

As I entered the dressing room, Destiny grasped my arms. Her brows knitted together. "Cherri! Hank told me what happened. Are you ok?"

I smiled. "Yes. I'm ok Destiny. Gunner – I mean, Ethan was there to stop Kyle from doing worse...."

She took hold of my jaw and moved my head from side to side inspecting my neck. "That fucking asshole! Well he's not allowed in here anymore. He's dangerous!"

"I know. Hank will not let him in here again after what he did to me. I feel better knowing that too." I fought back tears. What he did frightened me.

Destiny pulled me and wrapped her arms around me. Then the tears came. "I'm here girlfriend. Some men just can't handle all the beauty and warmth that is you. You wear your heart on the outside. And some men just want to fuckin take, take, take. And if you don't give it to them, it insults their ego."

It was finally Saturday morning. I dressed warmly, my hair in a ponytail, and ready thirty minutes before Ethan arrived. I pulled back the curtain at my front window the moment I heard the low rumble of motorcycle pipes. He was right on time. My jaw dropped at the sight of him, pulling up alongside the curb, and planting his black boots down in front of the house. He looked so sexy and dangerous sitting on that cherry red motorcycle wearing his leather club vest over a black and white plaid flannel shirt, his jeans fit snug to his thighs.

Trooper planted his front paws on the window sill and barked. "Yes Trooper, Ethan is taking me for a ride on his motorcycle today!" He tilted his head and whined, as his tail wagged.

I turned from the window to grab my leather jacket my clutch purse that I could sling across my chest and headed toward the door. But as I touched the door knob, I stopped. I didn't want to seem so forward and direct. The proper way was to greet your date at the door. So, I tossed my purse and jacket back on the couch and peaked out the window again. Just so I could watch his sexy walk toward my house. His confident swagger had a hint of pent up prowess and sexual energy, and my belly fluttered.

He knocked three times. I closed my eyes and exhaled and opened the door. His forearm leaned against the door frame. He slid his sunglasses down the bridge of his nose and the side of his mouth rose in a half smile. "Hey Gorgeous." His deep voice rumbled low like the sound of his motorcycle. He looked down. "Hey Trooper!" He pulled his shades back up and knelt down, petting Trooper's chest. Lucky dog.

As he stood back up, his eyes roamed down my body, and back up to meet mine, "Good. You're dressed perfect for the ride. You ready?'

"Yes!" I turned to fetch my jacket and purse – again - telling Trooper to be a good boy and locked up the house. I walked along beside Ethan, slinging my purse over my shoulder to fit across my chest.

"Looks like he's made himself at home with you, darlin."

"Yes. He seems happy with me."

"Why wouldn't he? He's a lucky fuckin dog if you ask me."

I couldn't help but giggle. "Well. I do spoil him. He sleeps at my feet on my bed."

"Again. Lucky fuckin dog."

His stare was so intense. I had to look away. "It's a beautiful motorcycle."

"Yeah. She's pretty."

"I like the color."

"Its my favorite." He was still looking at me, not his motorcycle. "Ok. So, let's get you zipped up."

AS I pulled on my jacket, fumbling with the zipper, his hands reached up and fastened it for me. He zipped it up, slowly, making my face flush, as he cleared his throat. He opened the compartment by the rear tire and pulled out a black helmet. "You'll need to wear shades. And this helmet." He placed it on my head and fastened the strap under my chin as I put on my sunglasses. "Now I'll get on first and stand the bike up. All you have to do is hold onto my shoulder and climb on behind me."

I did everything as he instructed, and it was easier than I thought it would be. The inside of my thighs hugged his hips. I got a very good look at the patches on his leather vest - CHAOS KINGS MC at the top and beneath it a skull wearing a horned Viking helmet on top of two crossed battleaxes. It took all the self- control I had not to arch my back and press my breasts up against his broad back.

He reached around, and took my hands, wrapping them around his waist. "Since this is your first time on a bike, I want you to hold on to me." He turned the key to the ignition and started the motorcycle. The seat suddenly vibrated to life. "Now when I lean, you lean *with* me. *Not* against me." He kicked what I looked like the gear shifter at his foot and we rode away from the curbside.

Sitting behind Ethan, with the vibrations of the motorcycle, felt like liquid warmth of arousal caressing my entire body. The chilly wind pushed against both of us as I clung to him. Everything around us was a fast moving blur. The sun was out with no clouds. I felt weightless, like flying at high speeds with invisible wings. The movement of Ethan's made the bike lean, and I leaned with him. He reached around with his left hand and slid it underneath my thigh and squeezed. His head swiveled toward me. "You're a natural darlin!"

"It feels natural. I feel free." Raising my voice next to his ear, above the sound of the loud thunder of the vibrating pipes.

We were surrounded by fall colored tree leaves of brown, red and gold, riding down backroads for about any hour. But it only felt like a minute, as he pulled up in front of my house again. And I didn't want the ride to end. He planted his feet down and turned the ignition off.

My arms were still wrapped around him. My cheek rested against his back. He reached up and covered my hands with his. They were a bit cold, as were mine. "We put in enough miles today for your first time, Fiona. Did you like it?"

"Did I ever! Can we do it again soon?"

He chuckled. "Yeah darlin. But I'm going to ease you into this. Slowly." His double meaning made me breathless.

I invited him in Trooper was there to greet us at the door, wagging his tail. His tongue was out panting and galloping in circles with so much excitement to see us return. We let him outside my fenced in backyard. Ethan scooped up an orange ball, one of the many toys that filled a bag he bought from the pet store and tossed it. Trooper's head tilted up to watch it arch toward the end of the yard. He trotted over, picked it up in his jaws and carried it back and Ethan tossed it again, and again. He turned, and his eyes met mine and his mouth curved up into a smile. It was contagious. He pulled out his pack of cigarettes and lit one.

"Thank you for the ride today. I really enjoyed it, Ethan."

"How long has that low-life scum been hurting you?"

The euphoric giddiness I felt suddenly disappeared and a stone landed in the pit of my stomach. "He's never physically hurt me like that before – "

"He's *been* hurting you. And I bet for a long while now."

"I don't think he will anymore. Not after how you stuck your gun into his mouth. "

"He's not allowed into the Cheetah anymore, Fiona. But I'm not going to underestimate him. Neither should you. Men like that don't let things go. I want you to be safe. I don't want you to be afraid."

I stepped toward him. "I'm not afraid *you* though."

His lips were suddenly mine then. I felt weightless as he bent and scooped me up into his strong arms. "Where's your bedroom?" his growl was low, his eyes so intense.

"Through the living room, down the end of the hall."

His mouth came crashing back down over mine again, driving his tongue to clash with mine. My hands raked through his dark messy hair. I moaned as he carried me through the hallway to my bedroom. He laid me onto the bed and covered me with his bulky frame. I opened my eyes when he pulled away from me. He pulled a black shear scarf hanging among other scarves on my bedroom door. "Close your eyes Fiona."

I sat up and closed my eyes. The scarf came over them. He wrapped it around my head and tied a knot. "I cannot look at you?" I stammered.

"No."

"But why – "

I felt his fingertips pressed to my lips, "Shhh. Just feel me." Then I felt his teeth and lips clamp down onto the crook of my neck – like he did at the bar. I cried out at the pressure of his bite. His hands began to unbutton my flannel shirt, his tongue sliding down my shoulder. He nipped and kissed along the way and yanked my bra cup down to expose my nipple.

"God Fiona. I'm consumed by you." My nipple was sucked into his mouth. I began to breath fast. He sucked and flicked his tongue back and forth over it. My hard little bud couldn't get any harder as it was teased by his hungry mouth.

His hands moved to my jeans. He unfastened them and pulled them down past my knees. His warm hand came over my mound. I cried out as two of his fingers glided down, in between my slit and buried themselves deep inside.

Then it happened. Flashbacks invaded my mind as my eyes were covered by the scarf. Darkness. Being closed in. The door locked from the outside. Four corners surrounded me. Squeezing me in. I was in in the closet again! I couldn't breathe! I sobbed and hiccupped, my bare ass raw and sore from the belt. My knees drawn up to my chest. My arms hugging my shins.

"No! Please stop!" I screamed, pulling Ethan's hand away from me. "I can't see! I can't breathe!" The scarf was suddenly pulled away from my eyes. I opened them to see Ethan's, his brows drawn together. "Ethan!"

He wrapped his solid arms beneath me and pulled me to his chest. "I'm sorry, Fiona." I started to sob into his flannel shirt and leather vest. 'It's ok. You're safe. You're here with me." He mumbled into my hair. "Will you forgive me?"

"There's nothing to forgive." My voice faint smothered into his shirt. "You didn't know."

He rolled onto his back, gathering me to lay on his chest. "What happened? Who hurt you?"

I never told anyone what happened. What my father did to me. If I never spoke of it, I could keep it buried deep inside, and left there, and only in my memories. I was afraid to speak of it, especially to a man who looked at me *without* disgust. "I was punished often for my wicked ways when I was young."

"Who punished you? You were young. How could anyone think you were wicked, darlin?" His voice cracked, deep and low.

"When the people you love keep telling you that, you start to believe it."

He huffed. "Your parents?"

"My father. He locked in a closet for hours to repent for my sins."

He hugged me tighter. His heart pounding hard against my cheek. "I'm so sorry that happened to you. I wish I could go back in time so, I could prevent all the pain that was done to you, Fiona. But from now on and every day after this one, I *will* protect you."

Those words meant so much to me. I smiled and rubbed my cheek against him. I breathed in the aroma of his leather vest, mingled with his own musky scent. And it calmed me. I did feel safe with him.

Gunner

I held Fiona in my arms for a long time and listened to her steady breathing as she fell asleep. But I was wide awake, starring up at motionless ceiling fan in the center of her bedroom. I just then remembered we left Trooper out in her backyard. I shifted my body out from under her. She didn't budge. I let him in and he jumped up, planting his paws on my thighs. Then he pushed off me and galloped down the hall into Fiona's bedroom. He was on her bed, licking her face by the time I caught up with him. I left Trooper with her, so she could rest up before she had to go to work at the Cheetah later that night.

I strapped my lid on, climbed back on my Road King and headed home. My grip on the bars were tight. I couldn't forgive myself for what I had just done to Fiona. I acted like a predatory animal only wanting to fulfill some kinky fetish without even considering how she would feel about being blindfolded. I moved way too fast and frightened her, making her remember the fucked up things she went through when she was young. I was only thinking about myself, not considering how covering Fiona's eyes in darkness would affect her, like all the darkness and pain in my head that could sometimes swallow me whole.

Fiona was so beautiful, she took my breath away. Her fiery red hair, her pale blue eyes, her creamy white skin and those rosy pink cupid doll lips. But what made her even more beautiful to me was her childlike innocence. She was also naïve and too trusting, even after what she told me about her childhood. She was an exotic dancer, with feline grace, revealing her gorgeous body with no inhibitions. I was obsessed with her. I wanted to protect her. Seeing blood, flesh and bone was just another day when I served in Iraq. I wanted to squeeze the trigger on my revolver I shoved it into Kyle's mouth. But I couldn't do that. Not in front of Fiona.

I took a long ride home to clear my head on that cool Saturday afternoon. It helped lift the heavy weight off my chest and subdue the throbbing headache. Even with the chill in the air, the sun was out as I moved rode through the wind. And it felt good. I realized then that Fiona was the only woman on this planet that took all that weight off me too. Her sweet velvety voice as she hummed to me. Like a cat purring. She was soft. And I wanted to be gentle and take things slow with her.

I didn't see Ratchet's truck, as I pulled up into the driveway into the garage. Both him and Sam were out running weekend errands, and Sam had to work a shift at the bookstore. I went down into my basement and there she was.

Gypsy. Curled up in a white fluffy ball on my pillow. She opened only one eye to peer at me as if to say, *"Thanks asshole. You just interrupted my sleep."*

"Not sure if you're going to be a good hostess to Trooper when he comes over to visit." She mewed at me.

Saturday night I played a game of pool at the clubhouse with my VP, Spider. And he was close to winning that game too. Skully and Tanya pulled up on his Super Glide. They were bundled up in their leathers as the temps had dropped and the afternoon sun had begun to hide behind the trees out in the parking lot. I took a bank shot to one of Spider's low balls and it rolled smoothly right into the corner pocket.

Skully sauntered up to us, in his unique gate because of his slight limp, as Tanya went to grab them both a beer from the bar. It had been a few months now and Skully's wounds healed up after Hammer beat the shit out of him. He had a scar now, down his left eyebrow from where Tanya's doctor stitched him up. He used to be a club member with those fucking women beaters, the Hell Hounds. But he proved himself and proved his loyalty to the Chaos Kings and Tanya. He was now a full patched in member of my tribe.

"Who's got high ball?" Skully asked as Tanya came up and handed him a beer.

I took another shot at one of Spider's balls, but my aim was a bit off and it didn't make it in the pocket. He took aim at one of mine now behind the cue ball, "Gunner does. And. Right about now. He won't have *any* balls." He pulled back the pool stick and struck the cue ball to my thirteen. It hit the bank and rolled all the way to the other end of the table and dropped in the corner pocket. The eight ball was last. Spider took aim. It was straight shot, dropping right into the side pocket.

Spider rose and turned to grin at me. "You're a better match for me, Gunner. Better than Wez or Magnet." He chuckled.

"Yeah. I'll second that motion."

Skully and Tanya started tonging each other in front of us, like they always did. It was never spoken, but the Chaos brothers knew Tanya called all the shots in that relationship. They were a good match though. And Skully's son, little Jake, was a good kid. He seemed to be easy going and liked to hang at the clubhouse sometimes, sitting on our bikes. He knew the rules though and would always ask first. He learned right away – you don't *ever* touch another man's bike, unless you ask first.

I walked back to the bar with Spider and left the lovebirds to their make out session. I grabbed a bottle of Petron from behind the bar and poured me and Spider a shot. He sat at the stool directly in front of me, lighting up a smoke. "You sure you wanna do a shot this soon? The night's early man."

"Need it now Spider. I'll keep it at a steady pace." We both downed our shot glasses. Spider slammed his back on the bar. I wiped my mouth with my flannel shirt sleeve and poured myself another. "I'm going to swing by the Cheetah later."

He exhaled a drag of his smoke. "So you seeing that redhead? What do they call her there?"

"Cherri. Her real name is Fiona."

"So, how's it goin with Fiona?"

"Good. I took her out for a ride on the bike. It was the first time on one. She was a natural though. Relaxed."

"That's good brother. She's really a pretty gal."

"Yeah she is. Not sure what she sees in me though."

Spider titled his head, his eyes scanning from my face, and down to my chest and cut. "You aint too shabby man. And you aint no asshole either."

"Ah. Whatever. If nothing else, I'm watching over her."

"Why's that? Someone bothering her?" He titled his head again, peering at me "Now Gunner, don't let that rage you keep all bottled up erupt from the inside."

"I won't. Fiona helps calm all that fucked up shit I deal with in my head. I like being with her. Some limp dick asshole has been stalking her and doing some fucked up shit. I almost put a bullet through his throat the other day."

"What did he do to her?"

"I came around the corner at the Cheetah, heading toward the VIP rooms and the motherfucker came out of a room and grabbed her by the throat. Pushed her up against the door. I scared him off with my revolver."

"Fuck, man." He shook his head.

"Not only that, he had a dog locked up in his shiny BMW, windows up, no AC. It was as hot as the Iraqi dessert – maybe hundred and thirty fuckin degrees in that car! I got my crowbar and smashed in a window. Got the dog out. He's shacked up with Fiona now. I call him Trooper."

"Fuckin A! Some shit-bags feel like they're a man when they hurt a woman, or an animal. It just shows how weak they are. They just need to stay way clear of this tribe, brother. I know people over at the County sheriff's department. Hell, some are my kin! What's this shit-bag's name? I could get some intel on him for you." Spider was a brother you could count on. That's why he was the VP of the Chaos Kings.

"Kyle is all I know. And his tag number. Easy to remember, 'CHA-CHNG'."

"That's all I need, Gunner." Spider's sly grin was contagious.

Fiona

All the dancers at the Cheetah were gathered together in the backstage dressing room. Larry, the owner walked in, followed by Hank, his huge frame coming through the doorway. Hank stood behind him, his bulky arms crossed over his chest, and mouth was set in a straight line.

Larry was a middle aged man. A short pudgy man, with kind eyes that crinkled at the corners. He ran a hand up to his balding scalp, imagining hair that was long gone. His eyes didn't meet any of ours, as he looked down at the floor. "Girls. I don't want to have to do this. But I'm selling the Cheetah. The paperwork will be done and made legit in a few weeks."

"But why Larry? You've owned this club forever!" Destiny was the first to protest.

Larry's eyes turned to her. "I'm sorry sweetheart. But I've been squeezed out. Nothing I can do about it. If I don't sell, then people will get hurt. Or worse."

"Who's squeezing you?"

"All you need to know is that you can stay on and dance here." Larry's mouth lifted in a smile, but his eyes were still sad. "And if you do, just be careful. I'm out and Hank's coming along with me. He won't be here to protect you."

"I wouldn't work for those Russian pieces of shits. They would just have to put a bullet in my head –" Hank grumbled.

Larry spun around, "Shut up. Not in front of the girls." He shuffled past Hank, leaving us.

We all stood silent. I felt my chest tighten and a churning in my stomach, full of anxiety. Hank unfolded his arms from his burly chest. "Larry is too scared. Worried about you girls and his own family. He's already been threatened, so I'm going to tell all of you now – don't stay. You don't want to rub up next to these Russians. They're snakes."

It was my turn on the stage and my movements were slow and languid in rhythm to the slow Audioslave song. I performed my back hook spin, placing my hand at the top of the pole and my other straight out across my chest. I walked around in rhythm to the haunting beat of the song and turned to face the opposite direction. I swung my inside leg forward and then back to hook it on the pole at my knee. I used my momentum and spun my body round and round. My red sequence pasties glittered with the reflection from the rotating disco ball that hung above me in the ceiling. I brought my outside leg up, bending it to put both my feet together.

But my heart felt heavy with sadness, and my performance fell flat. The Cheetah was busy as usual on a Saturday night, with customers at the bar and at the tables around the dancefloor. My eyes surveyed the club and I looked toward the corner of the club. And the same exhilarating sight greeted me – Gunner sitting alone at his table, arms folded, his hand wrapped around a glass of whiskey.

Chris Cornell's deep melancholic voice ended, and the song was over. "Give it up for Ms. Red Hot Cherri fellas!" Jay Jay came over the microphone. I stepped down off the side of the stage, wiping the sweat from the back of my neck with a towel.

And Ethan was there, at my side. He didn't touch me, but his eyes were stern, and his brows knitted together "Let's go to the VIP. Now." His warm hand was on the back of my elbow, but he led the way down the hall to one of the rooms not being occupied.

I walk in first, and followed, shutting the door. He leaned up against it, folding his arms across his chest, "Did you see those big men out there wearing suits? One of them smoking a cigar?"

I did notice them. "Yes I saw them. Why?"

"They're Russian. The criminal kind."

I tossed the sweaty towel on the couch. "Yes. Larry just told all of us tonight that he is selling the Cheetah. To those men out there. He didn't' say much, only that we need to be careful."

He stepped a few paces towards me. He was so close I craned my neck up to meet his dark eyes. He grasped my arms. "Fiona, you're not working here anymore."

"But I haven't had time to think about what I'm going to do, Ethan! I've worked here for so long. It's the money that I can make here to able to live on my own. Away from my parents. Away from Kyle and not having to depend on him."

He went silent, his eyes bore into mine. "You don't know what these Russians are about Fiona, so I'm going to tell you. My brother, Ratchet. You remember him from the patch in party here? His ole lady, Sam. She was property of the Hell Hounds MC. They're a diamond club. Outlaw. A bunch of low-life dirty hounds who'd sell their own mothers! So much violence was done to her. She was abused. She was raped. Over and over. She was used to do other depraved things that I can only imagine. The Hounds planned on selling Sam to those same Russians sitting out there right now. They're in the business of human of trafficking, Fiona. And other things. I'm sure of it. But luck was on our side and we got Sam out of the MC and we saved her from being sold as a sex slave! And that's why you are not working here anymore. As of right now!"

All the things Ethan just said terrified me. My heart pounded fast in my chest and I felt a flush of anxiety rush up my body. I suddenly felt cornered. Trapped. Inside that dark closet. My only reaction was to lash out of what was right there in front of me. "And what about the Chaos Kings MC? Aren't all your kind just gangsters too? Is this woman, Sam, now the property of the Chaos Kings MC?"

I expected my words would make Ethan flinch and move away from me. But he pulled me roughly up against his chest instead. His strong hand reached up to the back of my scalp. He gripped my hair close and I gasped as my neck was suddenly tilted back. "No Fiona. The Chaos Kings are not like them. We don't hurt anyone, man, woman, like some monsters do in this world. We are our own Tribe. We take care of our own. And I'm going to take of you from this very fucking moment on." His mouth came crashing down roughly on mine. and invaded my lips with his tongue.

I pulled away him. "I don't want to be in the dark anymore, Ethan! Don't shut that door on me! Let me in!" I pressed my hands against his hard chest.

His brows knitted together, and he squeezed his eyes shut. He balled his fists and smashed them against his temples. "I'm messed up in here, Fiona. That desert was Hell. Literally. I Fought alongside my brothers and sisters in the War over in Iraq. I was Sergeant in the Army, and the Gunner on an Abrams tank, and I served in a Platoon. It was home to me, along with my Tank Commander, Driver, and Loader. And now I battle PTSD every fucking day. I have flash backs and headaches. I don't sleep much either. I break out in a cold sweat sometimes, and don't even know what triggers it. It just happens. My mind is fucked up." He opened his eyes and he glared back at me. "Not only that, I'm filled with pent up rage. Like thrashing around in a cage. I sometimes only see darkness, tunnel vision."

My heart skipped a few beats. I reach up and caressed his cheek with my fingertips. "You are so very handsome to me, Ethan. I see darkness too, all the time. And I fear it too." He closed his eyes again and groaned.

He took both my hands and stepped back a few paces, pulling me with him. He sat down on the red velvet couch, planting me down on his lap, my thighs straddling his hard muscular thighs. "Dance for me, darlin."

I began to slowly swivel my hips, grinding and gyrating on top of his now rock hard manhood. I flipped my hair in rhythm to my swiveling hips. He lifted his hips and unzipped his jeans. He yanked them down, along with his boxers. "You're on top so you have all the control. Take as much of me as you can, darlin." His deep and hungry voice was strained as he gritted his teeth.

I was already slippery wet and reached down between us to pull my thong to the side. Then I slowly lowered myself on him. The thickness of his smooth head stretched me. He hissed and clenched his jaw, trying to maintain control to let me do as I pleased. "God Fiona. We need to take this as slow as you need." I bit my bottom lip as I inched down a bit more, filling myself up with his massive cock.

I gasped as I felt my core stretch even more but couldn't go any further. And he was only half way in. He clutched my hips and prevented me from moving. "That's enough. This time. Next time I'll go deeper." I broke his hold and began to move up and down slowly on hard length. I cried out again and began to rub my swollen clit. The pace of my breathing sped up, almost to panting. I was on the brink of an intense orgasm. And then it happened. I cried out as my core exploded with a burst of hot molten pleasure.

"That's a girl. Come all over me!" His masculine voice rumbled. I rode him, spasming around his cock and came crashing over that pinnacle of pleasure.

"Watch me," he growled as he lifted me off him. I stood above him and watched as he gripped his bold and slick manhood with both hands, twisting and pumping. His roar was primal and fierce as milky white cum gushed from his magnificent erection.

His body shook, while his hands still gripped his spasming cock. I climbed back on him, straddling his lap, and wrapped my arms around his broad shoulders. Then I began to hum for him. I was out of tune and the melody was simple, but he seemed to like it as he steadied his breathing. I caught the scent of our mingled sex as he leaned his forehead into my breasts and wrapped his strong arms around me.

We held each other for a few moments, to calm our pounding hearts. Ethan was a sexual beast. I felt his dominating essence whenever I was near him. He said he wanted to take care of me. No man had ever said that to me before. They just wanted to take *from* me, or hurt me, or keep me in closed in darkness that could swallow me whole. And Ethan saw darkness too. But if he kept me in the light and allowed me to see him, I would do whatever he wanted of me to help soothe his broken mind.

"I don't know what I'm going to do now," I mumbled.

He leaned back, cupping my face with his warm hands. His eyes were half closed with a relaxed glossiness to them. "We'll think of something darlin." I leaned down and kissed him.

I left the VIP with Ethan to pack my things in the dressing room and to let Larry know I wouldn't be coming back tomorrow night. I hugged Destiny before we started to pack our things. We were both in tears. Mine were for all the anxiety I felt, not knowing how I was going to pay my bills.

Destiny's tears came, but she was full of anger. "Just when things are good, a bunch of no good, mobbed up assholes have to come in here and fuck everything up!'

"Destiny! Don't say those things," I whispered. "They are sitting out there now! Ethan knows about them. They are very dangerous men. Stay away from them!"

"I don't give a fuck! Those kinds of men keep people like us down! Stepping on us. Crushing us. Fucking us. They just lust over power and greed! And we're just trying to make a living!" Her eyes suddenly shifted to something behind me.

"Such a dirty mouth on a pretty girl..." The deep male voice had a thick accent. I turned to see a huge man, as big as Hank smiling back at both me and Destiny. He was dressed in a charcoal grey expensive looking suit, with a cigar clasped between his fingers in his hand. A haze of cigar smoke surrounded him as he winked at us. "Your mouth should be put to better use, little lamb."

He frightened us both. Destiny turned back and knelt to gather her bag, acting as if she ignored him. She pulled me in for another tight hug. "Stay close to that biker man of yours, Fiona. I'll catch up with you later." She walked past me toward the Russian man. He stood still, blocking her path toward the door. He chuckled then, shoving the cigar in his mouth and stepped aside. She hurried past him quickly. He winked at me, then turned to follow her.

I rushed toward the door and slammed right into a hard chest. "Whoa darlin!" Ethan. Thank goodness. I dropped my bag and clung to him, sobbing.

He wrapped his arms around me and held me tight. "Shhh. I'm here. Let's go."

Apprehension and unease had a grip on my insides as I drove home. Like I was hanging off a cliff, not knowing what was below, and only saw darkness. Walls closing in around me and I couldn't see what was in front of me, or above me. Ethan followed me in his truck and carried my duffle bag into the house. Trooper greeted us both, Ethan kneeling to ruffle with his jowls as was now the ritual when they greeted each other.

"Will you stay for a while?" I mumbled. He looked up into my eyes from where he knelt.

Standing up he cupped my cheek. "Of course Fiona." I closed my eyes and nuzzled into his warm hand.

Ethan cradled me in his lap for a nice long while and just held me as she cried. He helped calm my fears just as I calmed the throbbing pain in his head. He whispered sweet things to me, and planted kisses to my ear while stroking my hair. My eyes grew heavy, and then I felt weightless. I wrapped my arms around his neck as he carried down the hallway into my bedroom. But when he lowered me onto the bed, my eyes flew open. I grabbed onto his forearms. "Don't go away!"

"I'm not going anywhere, darlin. But you need some sleep. I'll come by tomorrow. I'll leave my number, so you can add it to your phone later. Now get some rest and call me later when you wake up." He pulled the blankets up over me and kissed my forehead. Trooper was on the bed, curled up down by my feet.

Kyle

I smashed up my ignition switch in the BMW using a brick. And as always, I thought up a good story for that boring wife of mine, about how the car was stolen in a bad area outside the neighborhood and suburbs where we lived. She wasn't going to know about that fucking dog that I wasted a few god-damn thousand bucks on. But I could see the hint of suspicion in Maggie's eyes, for a brief moment, before it was gone. She knew not to question me. Ever.

I sat in my office with the door shut and got Marco on the phone, filling him in on what happened to the fucking dog he sold me.

"That sucks, but I can't help you out man. Deals a deal. You're a dumb shit for leaving the damn dog in your car-"

I clicked the red hang up button on the cell and threw it, smashing it against the wall. I clenched my hands into fists. Rage and adrenaline rushing through me. Even though I paid way too much for the damn thing, it was going to make some money for me in the dog fighting business. That way I'd be able to pay off my gambling debts to a few sleazy business men I owed money to. The day job just wasn't paying what I deserved. And Maggie was worthless when it came to being the wife I expected her to be; no skills, no intelligence and no sexual appeal at all.

Fiona. I could see her when I squeezed my eyes shut. That whore knew how she affected me. She tempted me time and time again. I was the one who took her in when she needed help and a place to stay. She came on to ME! She used her sultry voice and batted her crystal blue eyes, tempting me every time she had the opportunity. My stupid wife was totally oblivious. And I offered her so many things to keep her happy, and to be with me. I would have even fucked her really good, the way a woman like her needed!

But then she rejected me and spread her legs for every man that she rubbed up against while she danced at that strip club. Now she was fucking some greasy redneck biker! She was just as depraved and sinister as those bikers were. She bewitched him too, just as she did me. I bet Fiona was sexually aroused watched him pull a gun on me.

I planned on getting the dog back, with Marco's help. And I knew how to convince Fiona that she belonged to me.

Gunner

Fiona called me a few hours later, her velvety soft voice coming through the phone. She talked to her landlord and got her rent paid up for the next few months until she could find another job. I reassured her that she wouldn't have to worry about anything, that I'd help her out if money got tight. I didn't tell her, but she knew I wanted to take care of everything for her.

Ratchet sat at the clubhouse bar with me, while Sam, Tanya, and Skully played a round of cutthroat at the pool table. "So how was your date? "

"It was really good. Took her for a ride on the Road King. The temps were a bit low. More reason for her to snuggle up against me." I smiled, remembering the feeling of her warm and soft body against my back. "It was her first time on a bike, but she was a natural."

He chuckled, and I didn't expect his hard left jab into my shoulder. "That's good brother. You broke her in. Once you get a chick on a Harley, its smooth sailing from there."

I starred at my beer bottle, peeling the label with my thumb. "Don't know about the smooth sailing. She hasn't told me much about her past, but from what I *do* know, she had it rough with her father growing up."

"I know the feeling." Ratchet tilted his bottle and guzzled. I knew about his past with his dear ole dad and the loss of his mother to suicide.

"How did you do it with Sam? She had a really fucked up life with the Hounds. I mean, how did you help get her out of her shell?" I looked over Sam shaking her hips and cheering as the pool shot she took at one of Skully's balls as it dropped into the corner pocket.

The corners of Ratchet's eyes crinkled, and he smirked at her. She winked back at him. "Yeah. Well. She escaped her hell. I was just there to catch her and lift her back up," he turned back to his beer, "but I don't think it's your girl that needs help out of her shell though."

"What's that supposed to mean?"

"Don't get all defensive. It's supposed to mean you, Gunner."

I turned back and continued to peel the label because I didn't want to agree with him. "I'm doing what the doc ordered. I'm taking the meds. And Fiona helps me with the headaches."

"Fiona huh? Nice name. You're lucky brother."

"Lucky?"

"Yeah. Lucky. You've got a good set of parents. Your father didn't bash your face in like mine did every other fuckin day. And your mother seems like a good woman. Like my mother. When was the last time you saw them? Talked to them? What about your little sister? Gabby right?"

Ratchet was right. Again. It had been a while since I talked to my parents and Gabby, let alone see them. I skipped out on last year's visit to them during the holidays too. And still felt some guilt over it.

"They are proud of you. Chaos is proud of you. I'm fucking proud of you. You were a bad-ass gunner on that Abrams tank in Iraq. You're an American hero, like all your brothers and sisters you fought along with over there."

"But I'm not the same person I was before I went. Flashbacks fuck my head all up. And the headaches too. Sometimes I feel the rage burning me up from the inside. In the pit of my stomach. I know I came back breathing and some of my brothers and sisters didn't. There's some guilt over that too. And it continues to eat at me."

"That moment when you signed up with the Army were willing to die too, damn it. You completed your mission and your duty. So, you need to lift that weight of guilt off your shoulders. What did you tell me that once?"

"What's that?"

"You were by my side when I tried to get Sam back. You would've put a bullet in the back of that sleezy fuck's head at the Steel Cage, if he put one in mine. Remember that? And you helped me get my little rabbit back and talked me out of going bat shit stupid and killing Sid and all his dirty dogs. You told me I did the best I could for my mother. That I was the best thing that ever happened to Sam. Well you're the best thing for us too. All of us. Your brothers and sisters in the war and Chaos. And your mom and dad, and sister. Your family. "

I swallowed down the last of my beer and tossed the bottle over the bar into the trash dumpster "Well. Baby steps brother. Fiona's on her way here now actually."

Ratchet's eyebrows lifted. "Oh is she now?"

I leaned away from him. "No more shoulder jabs man. Yeah. I want her to come meet Chaos. But this time with her clothes on instead of just a g-string. And you'll get to meet Trooper too. He's coming along with her."

"Who's Trooper?"

I chuckled as Ratchet's brows bunched up, looking all "protective caveman" like he did when it came to Sam. "You'll see. He watches over Fiona. You'll like him."

Skully missed his shot at the pool table, the cue ball rolling in between the two he aimed for as Fiona came walking in, her thick locks of long red hair bouncing on her shoulders. Trooper trotted along beside her. She had that affect on any male within her vicinity. She sauntered over to me, wearing a studded black leather jacket. Her tight low-cut black tank top directed my eyes to that tantalizing cleavage. Her jeans were tight as fuck, outlining her shapely hips and ass. Her stiletto black boots covered her toned calves up to mid-thigh.

I was tongue tide so all I could mumble was, "whoa", as she wrapped her arms around my neck. I got a whiff of the leather jacket mingled with her own scent. Honeysuckles. I couldn't help myself and seized her curvy hips with my hands. I leaned back to let my eyes have their way with her body, biting down on my lower lip.

Ratchet cleared his throat, interrupting my trance she just put me in. I looked over at him and smirked. "You remember Fiona?"

He nodded his head and tipped his beer bottle to her. "Hey Fiona. Ratchet."

Fiona stayed in my arms, and titled her head, beaming a smile at him. "Hi Ratchet. I remember you from the party you had a few months ago at the Cheetah."

Trooper hiked his paws up onto Ratchet's lap, his tongue hanging out the side of his mouth. It made him look like he was grinning. "This must be Trooper." Ratchet reached out his hand to introduce himself by scent. Trooper licked it and wagged his tail. "He probably smells Gypsy all over me."

The sun went down early since the fall season was here. The temps dropped along with it, as the night got started at the clubhouse. Tanya and Sam warmed up to Fiona and fluttered her around the clubhouse like little butterflies, introducing her to some of the other women. The three of them chirped like little birds, and everyone gave off a friendly vibe toward her. I shared another shot of whiskey with Ratchet, as Trooper sat right at my feet beside my barstool.

The warm effects of the whiskey kicked in as I watched Fiona every moment she was not within reach. She would look over at me often and smile, batting her sexy pale blue eyes at me. Magnet showed up with his two women, Brandy and Becky, attached to each side of him, his arms draped over both of them. I needed to be next to Fiona. Trooper followed right beside me as I ambled up behind her as she talked to the B girls. I caught her honeysuckle scent again and wrapped my arms around her middle, pulling her up against my chest. Magnet sported a crooked grin as I nodded my head to him. I didn't feel the same vibe his girls gave off like the others. They both liked to be the center of Magnet's attention, along with all the other club members. And maybe they felt a bit more competitive around my sexy red haired witch.

Fiona

I was so thrilled but anxious when Ethan invited me to the Chaos Kings clubhouse. I couldn't wait to see him again. But as I walked in with Trooper by my side, my knees went weak at the sight of him. He was sitting at the bar with a man as handsome as he was, but with a bit more of a brooding expression. I realized then that Ethan's beard had grown a bit longer. He wore his leather vest over a black and grey plaid flannel shirt, and it unbuttoned to reveal a hint of his tattooed chest. His eyes were focused on my walk, his jaw hung open, which gave me a happy confirmation that what I wore had that affect that I hoped to achieve. And his eyes had the same affect on me, making my heart pound hard in my chest, and flutters erupt in my stomach.

Sam and Tanya were very warm and friendly. Sam was a petite brunette, her pouty mouth giving her a look of innocence. But her captivating smile lit up her adorable face. Tanya was simply gorgeous, with sandy blond hair and high cheek bones. She wore a tight neon pink tank top, which showed off her fiery amber colored eyes. The President's wife, Madge, was warm and welcoming as well. She had that matriarch vibe, with her jet black Bettie Page hairstyle and red lipstick, and her red painted fingernails. She had many tattoos, even on the tops of her hands, decorated with floral designs. The women made me feel more comfortable and helped settle my nervousness. This was my first time standing around a bunch of bearded bikers, who gave off that testosterone unfused presence that was totally primal. And all male. Most of them had so many tattoos, from shoulders, to biceps, to forearms. Some even had detailed designs on their necks!

Clouds of cigarette smoke and the sweet scent of marijuana wafted through out the clubhouse. Ethan guided me, placing his hand on the middle of my back. He leaned down close to my cheek and mumbled that it was time to introduce me to his brothers. I met the President, Rocky. He was similar in size as Ratchet – huge and bulky. He looked to be in his early forties, with a bald head, a goat-tee beard and covered in tattoos all over his shoulders and arms. He pulled me in and smacked a kiss on my cheek. Then I met Spider, the Vice President. He was very tall, with dark hair that grew past his shoulders and braided, with a trimmed beard. He had a warm handsome smile, shaking my hand and giving me a wink. I was introduced to all the other men and was pleasantly surprised to feel welcomed with their polite head nods and huge pawlike handshakes from some.

"What's your favorite go-to drink, darlin?" Ethan's warm hand still was splayed on the middle of my back, as we walked together back to the bar where Ratchet had just left. I climbed onto his stool as Ethan walked around to other side of the bar.

"My devil juice is rum, but I'll just have beer tonight." I winked at him as he grabbed two bottles from a bar ridge, twisted the cap off and handed me one. We bumped them and took a drink of the nice cold beer.

He came back around to sit next to me. "I'm glad you came Fiona. I wanted you to meet my Chaos brothers, and some of the women. They call themselves the Chaos Coven. Remember, we're not outlaw. And are a close knit. It's tribal. We take care of our own." His deep voice smooth, giving me a tingling up my arms and over my nipples. "And we don't hurt women." He looked away, lifted his bottle and took another drink.

"I'm sorry for saying those things to you about your club. They are your family. I see now how important they are to you, Ethan."

"Nothing to apologize for. You're important to me too. That's why I wanted you here with me tonight. You can be yourself here. Be who you *want* to be. No one here will judge you." I was transfixed by his sexy dark eyes as he leaned down and brushed his warm lips against mine. Then his mouth curved into a warm handsome smile.

I couldn't help but smile back at him. "Drinking, dancing and fornication are sinful and wicked, according to my father."

"Then let's be sinful and wicked together. My beautiful vixen..." He leaned into me again, his mouth crashing against mine. Not so sweet and soft, but rough this time. It was barbaric, like he claimed me for himself. His skillful tongue plunged between my lips, lashing at mine.

Nice warm giddiness filled me up inside as I sat with Ethan at the clubhouse bar talking and laughing. Trooper was such a devoted canine who stayed alert but relaxed by our feet. Ethan reached down to ruffle Trooper's ears. He looked up at him, wagging his tail, his long tongue hanging out the side of his jaw.

A man I recognized from the Cheetah hollered over to Ethan, "Hey Gunner! I need some competition over here! I just ripped Skully a new asshole." The man looked very intimating, with a peculiar hair cut shaped in a mohawk, but began to grow out. He was covered in tattoos and the sound of his voice was deep, sounding more like a growl.

Ethan chuckled. "You sure you want a piece of me?" He climbed off his stool and offered his hand to me, smirking.

"Come on with me. You wanna watch me kick the ass of the King of kink, at a game of pool?"

I took his hand. "Sure. You can teach me. I've never played pool before."

His brows shot up. "Oh really?" Then he winked. "I'll remedy that here for you. Right here and right now, darlin."

When Ethan introduced me to Wez, he reached out and gave me a big bear hug, lifting me off my feet, and gave me a loud smacking kiss on my cheek. "He's the one you need to watch, Fiona." Ethan grumbled, but his eyes wrinkled at the corners, showing me that he was joking. I watched him as he set up the pool balls on the red felt table by placing them into a triangular grouping with what he called a rack. Wez stood at the other end of the table and thrusted his pool stick at the white cue ball. It struck hard against the tight group of multi-colored balls and they rolled and scattered and bumped into on another. Ethan explained to me that the strategy was to knock all of Wez' balls into the pockets, and that the black eight ball goes in last. Ethan had the solid colors and Wez had the striped colored ones.

The game over a in just a few minutes as Ethan shot the black eight ball into a corner pocket. Wez shook his head, walking away. "Just gotta show off in front of your beauty, don't you brother..."

Ethan shrugged his shoulders, turning to me and smirked. He beckoned me with his forefinger, his eyes gleaming. "Come over here darlin. I'll teach you my ass kicking slick moves."

He did the same as before, racking the balls, and breaking them from the other end of the table. He handed me the pool stick, his eyes glued to mine, and moved to stand very close behind me. He reached up and grasped my forearms, pushing me to lean over the table. I arched my back a bit, raising my ass to bump against his hard crotch. He nuzzled his rough bearded cheek against mine and inhaled. "Never thought I'd have a raging hard on while playing a game of pool. But then I never had someone as fucking delicious as you rub up on me like this."

I turned my head toward him. "I just can't help myself," my husky voice brushed against his rough cheek.

I tried to focus on what Ethan was teaching me, how to hold the stick, how to aim at the cue ball and how hard or soft to thrust when taking my shot. But I was distracted more than anything, by his voice deep and how his eyes stayed with mine while he instructed me. He went back to the bar and brought back two shot glasses, handing me one. I tilted it up and emptied it in one swallow. My eyes widened as I coughed.

Ethan downed his then, and chuckled. "You wicked girl."

The burning liquor slithered down my throat, down to my belly, making me flushed and warm. And aroused. "You haven't seen wicked yet. I feel like dancing. Right here on top of this pool table."

He took the glass and pool stick from me. "Then let's make that happen." I suddenly felt weightless as he lifted me with his strong hands. I planted my boots on the red velvet covered pool table, while hands slid down the sides of my thighs. "I'll go play something on the juke that you can dance to darlin."

Magnet's two girlfriends were the first to notice me standing on the table. They anchored their hands on their hips, their eyes glaring at me. I had seen that look many times from women before, and just ignored them. The sound of Rob Zombie 's dark voice and the steady sexy beat of a song began to play through the speakers in the clubhouse. I started to move my hips languidly, roaming my hands up from my stomach to my breasts, and pushing them together. My ass and hips always had a mind of their own, as they began to bump and grind to the striptease beat. All eyes in the clubhouse were on me. But my eyes were focused on Ethan. And only Ethan. He stood and watched me. His tongue darted out and swiped along his bottom lip, looking at me like he was going to devour me before the night was over.

Clapping, whooping and whistles erupted when the song ended. Ethan beamed a huge grin at me as he reached up to bring me down off the table. Ratchet's woman, Sam approached and leaned in toward me to whisper, "could you teach me how to dance like that?" Her faced suddenly blushed a shade of pink.

"Sure, I can Sam! It's not that hard. You just need to *feel* the music. Feel it with your body. "

She giggled. "OK I'll try. But don't tell Gunner…" Her blush suddenly disappeared, and her eyes met Ratchet's from the bar. His brows lifted with a questioning look. She winked back at him. "Ratchet gets my pulse racing all the time. So, I want to surprise him. To get his pulse racing as fast as mine." We traded phone numbers and planned to get together soon. I was happy at that moment. Another woman, besides Destiny, actually liked me.

As the night turned into early morning, everyone started to shuffle out of the clubhouse, or stagger down the hall, where I assumed the bathrooms were. "It's getting late. Some head home, some stay the night here. There's a few rooms down the hall where some can stay the night." Gunner began to gather the pool balls again, racking them together. It became all quiet in the clubhouse. No more music, no more sounds of the biker's laughter. "Let's play another game, then I'll drive you back to your place. You can leave your car here. I'll bring you back to get it in the morning."

But I didn't want to play pool anymore. I wanted Ethan. Right then and there. I suddenly had an idea and I couldn't help but grin. I told him I was going to break the seal, and he pointed toward hall telling me the bathroom were at the end. I disappeared for few minutes and came out, doing my sultry cat walk back down the hallway toward Ethan, and stopped. He was about to break a new game as I anchored a hand on my hip. He looked up then, to see me wearing my knee high stiletto boots. And nothing else. His aim was off. The white cue ball missed the multicolored grouping and rolled toward me and dropped into a side pocket.

Trooper sat on his haunches by the bar, tilting his head at me and whined. "Go take a piss outside, Trooper," Ethan barked at him, but his eyes still on me. And Trooper trotted his way out of the clubhouse.

I walked toward him as his eyes roamed down my body. Ethan dropped the pool stick and it clattered to the floor. He slid his leather vest off his shoulders, spreading it on the end of the table where he stood. By that time, I was only a few feet away from him. He reached out and snatched me by my hips, spinning around me to face the table. I planted my palms on his leather vest, as he pressed his chest up against my back and ass. He reached around and cupped my breasts with his strong warm hands. "Naughty girl." He slammed his hips into my bare ass. "*This* is what you do to me."

My breath hitched. He was hard as stone.

He leaned away. "Spread your legs for me." I did, arching my back, which raised my ass for him to devour with his eyes. He knelt, gripping my hips, and buried his face in between my ass. I braced my splayed hands on the velvet table top and heard him grunt as his lips smothered my moistened heat. I cried out as his tongue caressed and explored my center. His fingers squeezed my ass cheeks and I couldn't help but wiggle and squirm on his warm slick tongue. It continued to slide down and rub circles around my swollen nub. I moaned and shuddered as hot liquid pleasure spread from my center and I climaxed uncontrollably on his relentless mouth.

My breathing came out in quick pants as I turned to watch him stand. He unbuttoned and unzipped his jeans fervently and yanked them down with his boxers his knees. My eyes drank in the sight of him as he lifted his flannel shirt. His abs were taut and lean, and his sexy V shape directed my eyes lower to his bold manhood. He was so hard and enormous!

"You're wet and ready for me now, Fiona." He was right. He grasped my hips and slid himself so easily into me. He went slow as his bold cock invaded me inch by inch, until he was buried all the way. He pulled out slowly and rammed himself back in. I slapped my hand over my mouth to prevent my cries to escape. He suddenly stopped in mid-thrust. "No! Don't care if anyone hears us or sees us. You're going to scream as I fuck you the way you *need* to be fucked, Fiona!" I obeyed him, taking my hand away from my lips and cried out as he thrusted into me over and over again.

His leaned down and clamped his lips and teeth onto my shoulder. He sucked and bit down. His grunts and moans were muffled as I felt his massive cock pulsate. His growled and he pulled out of me. He suddenly flipped me around and lifted me up onto his leather vest on the pool table. "I want to look into your eyes as I come deep inside of you my beautiful witch!"

I cried out again as he plunged back into me, over and over again. We looked into each other's eyes as he suddenly roared and climaxed. I screamed out as his hot semen shot up against my core.

We were both breathless as he collapsed on top of me. Ethan pressed his sweaty forehead onto my chest as he wrapped his arms around me while we calmed our pounding hearts. He rose up, and pulled his jeans back up, and scooped my exhausted body up in his muscular arms, carrying me down the hallway. The room he took me to was dark, but I could make out a bed that he laid me on. I slide over a bit so Ethan could settle himself next to me.

"It's not the Ritz Carrolton, but it's clean and good enough for us tonight." He whispered low next to my ear. His fingers began to caress the outer curve of my breast. My nipple beaded up instantly to his warm touch. He inhaled deep and then chuckled low. "I could sink myself into you again right now…. But I'll let you rest. You've been very deliciously wicked for me tonight." I could only make out his beard covered jaw line and his profile in the light from the little lamp on a nightstand. I smiled lazily. He wanted me again just moments after he took me on that pool table. I felt sweet warm tingles through my limps and between my thighs.

Trooper trotted into the room and sat by the side of the bed looking up at Ethan. "She's mine tonight, Trooper." He whined, then curled up on the floor. "Soon we'll introduce Jake to Trooper. I think they'd get along really well."

"Who is Jake?"

"He's Skully's boy. He's a good kid."

"That's nice. Is Tanya his mother?"

"No. But she loves and dotes on him like a good mother does."

It made me think about my little brother, Seth. But he wouldn't be little anymore. I also thought of my own mother. How she tried as best she could to be a good mother to me and Seth. Tears began to well up and run down the corners of my eyes. Ethan rose up onto his elbow and brushed his calloused thumb down one of one of them, "Hey now darlin. What's wrong? You wanna tell me?"

I just couldn't keep it bottled up inside me any longer. I needed Ethan to hear my voice, and the know how it was like for me growing up. "For as long as I can remember, my father drank too much every day. He became a monster, shouting his bible verses and punishing me for things that he saw as sinful and wicked."

Ethan's head tilted. "Whatever could you done that was so sinful and wicked?"

"For dancing or humming along to music I played on my clock radio. Father told me, even when I was a little girl, that I tempted men because I was wicked. That I tempted him too…" Images of his hand sliding up underneath my pink dress as he made me sit on his lap. His rough calloused fingers touching my thighs. I shut my eyes tight to block out the horrible images. But I continued to let it all out to Ethan because I wanted to tell him everything, "He would touch me. I didn't want him to. But he told me he couldn't help himself. That is was my fault."

Ethan's brows bunched together, his eyes looked full of rage. "It was not your fault Fiona. You were innocent. He was a fucking monster that doesn't even deserve to breath!"

"So, I ran away. My father would stay sober for a few weeks at a time. But then something or someone would always trigger him to go on a day long drinking binge. Then the hate and anger would come out. He would beat me, or my mother and even my younger brother, Seth. "

"It was like any other night at my house. I worked at the local supermarket in town and I came home to see my father back hand my mother across her face. She fell onto the couch sobbing. I dropped to the floor on my knees at my father's feet and covered my mother from another blow. I begged and pleaded for him to stop. His blood shot eyes were full of hate, fear and rage. He grabbed a hold of me by my hair and dragged me down the stairs to the basement and locked me in that small dark closet, like he did so many times before. I heard my mother screaming upstairs as I sat in that closet in the darkness crying and suffered panic attacks."

Not long after, mother came down to the basement and let me out of the closet. More sounds of shouting and cursing came from upstairs. It was Seth and Father. The side of Mother's face was swollen and red. Red blotches that looked like handprints marked her forearms. She pulled me to her and shoved two thick rolled wads of cash into my hands. 'Take this money and get out of here Fiona. Take a bus and go to your cousin Kyle up north of town. You are not safe here anymore.'"

"We both jumped at the sound of Seth and Father yelling, then there was a loud thud. Mother grabbed me and held me tight. I clung to her and didn't want to let go as we both cried. I didn't want to leave, but mother was right. Father was dangerous. But I didn't want to leave her and Seth there.

We crept up the stairs together, and found Father was passed out on the floor. Seth was standing over him, his hands balled up into fists. He had just turned eighteen and grown taller. That was the first time he was able to knock Father out cold. Seth turned to look at both me and mother and told me to go, to leave now. I came to him and hugged him tight. He was trembling and his body full of pent up rage. He couldn't even hug me back. So, I hitched a ride to the bus station and got a one way ticket to leave the town I grew up in, and the only family I had."

"I lived with Kyle and his wife Maggie for about a year. Kyle is a distant cousin of mine on my father's side. He made me feel uncomfortable from the very first day I arrived. He would look at me the way my father looked at me. Like I was tempting him in some way. I then felt I was just that, a wicked sinful whore. But I loved to dance and sing, and it came naturally to me. So, I took a job at the Cheetah, so I could dance. I knew men looked at me as just an object, but I didn't care. I could dance to my heart's content and taught myself and trained my body to do those things I can do on that pole. Music is something you can feel, not just listen to. Larry paid us girls very well and Destiny has been a devoted friend to me since the day I set foot in the Cheetah. She's sassy and sometimes there is no filter when it comes to what she says. And I didn't have to worry about anyone hurting me or worry about unwanted touching from the men because Hank looked out for all of us."

Etan's brows knitted together, listening to me spill my life out to him. "Do you stay in touch with your mother and your brother?"

I felt a lump in my throat. "Yes. I send my mother cards and letters. That's the only way to stay in touch. Since I left, Seth got into violent fist fights with our father. He dropped out of high school and ran away. He reached out to my mother last year and he called me on a cell phone a few times. He didn't tell me where he was though, but I knew he was homeless and living on the streets, doing what he needed to do to survive. He called me several times more, but then I lost contact with him. Neither me or mother have not heard from him in over a year. My mother was the last to leave my father. She got a bus ticket out of Richmond like I did and ended up living with my Aunt Cheryl in South Carolina."

My voice faded. I couldn't tell Ethan anymore. He rose up over me. I spread my thighs for him and he settled himself between them. His hands slid into my hair and he captured my face in his hands, staring into my eyes. His were full of intense yearning and fiery need. "We both have been surrounded by that pitch black darkness. I struggle with the pain in my head and the PTSD. You were hated and abused by your own father. But as of now, when you feel you're in the dark, I'm right beside you. Don't ever be afraid. No one will hurt you anymore. Your father, Kyle, no one. Because your mine."

Gunner

I wore my gloves, leather jacket and chaps since there was a cold bite of wind against me as I rode my bike over to Fiona's house. Even with the cold, she still wanted me to take her for another ride and she told me she had some good news. Hearing her excited voice over the phone, always lifted the dark clouds in my head. I couldn't wait to see her, touch her, kiss her. I had to shift my hips on the seat then, because of a semi-hard on just thinking about it all the things I wanted to do to her.

As I made my turn at the stop sign a quarter mile from Fiona's house, the BMV with the "CHA-CHNG" tag was suddenly in my sights. It was parked along the side of the road in the quiet old neighborhood. That motherfucker was either stupid or brave! As I rolled toward the car, Kyle's eyes went wide when he saw me. I opened the throttle, revving so my pipes thundered, and pulled over in front of his car. I kicked my stand down, climbing off and rushed toward Kyle as he pushed his key fob. But I got to him before he could get in. My jaw was clenched so tight, the pain pounded in my temples as I grabbed the front of his suit jacket and slammed him up against the car.

"If you ever touch Fiona again, or even look her way," I hissed, "I'll get that dog you almost cooked in your car, to chew your fuckin balls off!"

Kyle grabbed at my fists that were gripped onto his jacket. "You vandalize my car, take my dog, and now you want to take my girl?"

I shook my head slowly, like I did the last time when he choked on the barrel of my gun. "She's not your girl. She never was. She's mine, motherfucker. Now get back in your car and get the fuck out of here!" I relaxed my grip on him and let go. I stepped back so he could open his door to get in, but my fists were still clenched, just waiting for some more dumb shit to come out of his mouth. But he didn't and drove off.

My blood pressure lowered as I pulled up in front of Fiona's house. Trooper darted out the front door as she opened it, trotting right up to me as I climbed off the bike. I ruffled his head and took off my lid and followed me back to Fiona. I grabbed her around the waist, lifting her up, as she wrapped her arms around my shoulders, and planted a hungry kiss on her soft plumps lips. I put her down and followed her into the house, Trooper leading us. "So, what's the good news darlin?"

She spun around, showing me a smile from ear to ear, her eyes gleamed with excitement. "I got a job! With Destiny!"

"That's great!" Of course, I wanted to know what that job was. "What's the job?"

Fiona turned to walk to her kitchen. "It's at Club Vibe. It's gentlemen's club. One of Destiny's cousins runs it. I'll be dancing with her." That's why she averted my eyes when she walked to the kitchen. She knew I wasn't going to like that idea.

"I'll help you find a decent job, darlin. Other than dancing. I don't want you dancing anymore."

She pulled her fridge door open, searching for something. She shut the door and turned to me. "That's what I'm good at Ethan. And I get paid *very* good money doing it. So that I can live on my own."

The throbbing pain started up again, pounding against my temples. Her eyes became wide as I marched toward her and gripped her forearms. She tried pulling away, so I seized her by the hips. "No Fiona. I mean, yes! You *are* a good dancer. But you're not doing it anymore. I don't want you alone with men in private rooms. You don't have to. And you don't have to worry about living on your own. I found you. And I'm going to take care of you."

"You sound like Kyle! You want to control me! Like I'm a nice new shiny motorcycle! Or some dirty plaything!"

Both her words and the pain in my head brought on the sweats. "You're not dirty, Fiona! And I'm not like Kyle! I give you what you need. Freedom to be who you want to be. Did you not like it when I fucked you on that pool table? Don't you know that I claimed you as mine right then and there?"

"I don't belong to you!" Her eyes fiery and wide. I slammed my mouth over hers, invading it with my ruthless tongue. She moaned into my mouth, but her hands were pushing on my chest, trying to break away. I leaned back, mesmerized by her pale blue eyes. "Maybe you don't feel it today Fiona. Maybe not tomorrow. But you *will* belong to me!"

She kept struggling against me. "No! leave me alone!"

I looked down at the sound of Trooper's whine. He was sitting right by my feet, his head titled. I let her go and she stepped away. I turned from her and left. I wasn't angry this time. And the pain that pounded in my head moved down to my chest as I climbed back on my bike and road away.

Fiona

The moment Ethan walked out of my house, my eyes welled up with tears. I couldn't stop them. But he made me so angry! At that moment, he made me feel like a *thing* to him, talking to me like he was going to call the shots in *my* life! That he owns me and that dancing for men in a private room was dirty and cheap.

I had been hoping he would have been happy for me. And even though the weather was getting a bit colder, I wanted him to take me for another ride on his bike that day. But those hopes and wants just didn't end up happening. I hadn't heard or received any text messages from him all day and there was a sinking feeling thumped in my chest for two longs days after he'd left.

I met Destiny at the Vibe on the third day. She brought me into the club's elaborate office and introduced me to her cousin, Markus. He was a cousin on her father's side of the family, a very handsome black man, with long dreadlocks with very similar features as Destiny, but more masculine. His smile was warm as he took my hand. "It's a pleasure Fiona. Destiny has told me only good things about you. You are a gem."

Destiny showed me around the club and the main stage. It was similar in size to the Cheetah with two other smaller circular stages on opposite ends of the club. The place was decorated red, silver and gold, with small tables and nice cushioned armchairs. The bar was lit up along the railing with neon pink lighting. The dressing room was basic with tables and mirrors and lockers.

Destiny was beaming as she showed me around and introduced me to the other dancers and bartenders "Markus couldn't wait to meet you after I showed him some pics of you Fiona. And he pays the dancers and all the staff good. Of course, you keep every tip you make. "

"Why have you not worked for him before?"

"Oh, I did a few years back before I went to the Cheetah. There was as some family drama going on between Markus and my uncle, his dad. Father and son bullshit. Anyway, I wanted to stay out of it for a while, and broaden my horizons, as they say. But now that Larry is selling out to those fucking slave traffickers, I'm never setting foot in the Cheetah again! So, I called Markus up to get the DL about him and his father, and they settled that shit between them. So, I'm back!"

I was staring at Destiny, but my mind was elsewhere. She waved her hand in front of my face, bringing be back. "You ok hon? You blanked out on me."

"Yes. Well, no."

"What's bothering you baby. Talk to Destiny."

I choked back the tears and swallowed the heavy lump in my throat. "Gunner. I mean Ethan and me. He tried to dictate me about how I make my living when I told him I got a job here at the Vibe with you. First, he told me he didn't want me to give private dances anymore. And that he wants to take care of me. Own me. Then I shouted at him to leave me alone." I tried to keep them at bay, but the tears flowed again.

"Fiona. Is he good to you?"

"Yes. He is. He doesn't judge me. He treats me with admiration. Like I'm equal to him. He touches me the way I like to be touched. And the way he kisses me. It makes me breathless."

Destiny grinned. "Then that's a *good* thing! Sounds like he's done more than admire you baby. Most men just want the booty and have a good time. And some are worse and treat you bad. And when I mean bad, I mean shitty bad! Your biker man scared the shit out of limp dick Kyle. That was so fucking hot! I wish I had a man that would pull out a gun on someone for me! That's not just admiration or obsession Fiona. That sounds like *love* to me."

Ethan loved me? I never thought a man would ever love me! Want me, or use me, yes. But love me? "But I hurt him when I screamed at him to leave me alone. He has not text or called me since."

She pulled me into her arms and squeezed. "We say things sometimes to hurt others. Love is a fucking scary thing, Fiona." She pulled back, "Now you call your biker man and make up with him. Because you know, make up sex is the best kind!" Her smile was contagious. I hugged her back. Destiny wasn't just stunningly gorgeous. She was wise and the best friend I ever had.

The heavy weight in the pit of my stomach lifted as I left the Vibe and headed home. I wanted to call Ethan, to apologize and tell him that I didn't mean what I said that day. When I entered my house Trooper greeted me, wagging his tail and barking a welcome home. "I'll give Ethan a call, so he can come over and toss that ball for you sweet boy." He barked again, like he acknowledged what I just said, making me laugh. But then he suddenly turned and galloped down the hallway to my bedroom.

"Trooper?" I followed after him. That's when I heard snarling and barking.

I stopped dead in my tracks. Kyle appeared from my bedroom, walking toward me, holding a gun, aimed at me. His eyes were bloodshot, but he smiled. "Hello Fiona. "

From behind him was a Latino man, with jet black hair. He had Trooper with a wire loop wrapped around his neck, attached to a long restraint bar. Trooper barked and growled relentlessly the man gripped both hands on the bar.

I stepped back a few paces to keep my distance from Kyle, but he kept coming toward me, "How did you get into my house?" He nodded his head to the man behind him, "My friend Marco here knows how to get into bedroom windows." His eyes pivoted to look over my shoulder behind me, "Where's your white trash biker boyfriend?"

Kyle gripped the gun tight, keeping it pointed at me. I began to shake. I felt adrenaline rush throughout my body and became dizzy and lightheaded with fear. "We broke up Kyle. I told him to leave me alone."

He laughed nervously. "Bullshit!" He barked. "Now I want you to call him *now*! And tell him to come here. Me and Marco here are going to have a talk with him."

I jumped at the hard pounding at my front door, "Fiona! Open the fucking door!" It was Ethan! Trooper kept barking and Kyle was on me then, colliding into my back and wrapping his arm around my waist. He pressed the gun to the side of my head, and pushed me forward. "Open the door Fiona."

Kyle stepped with me to the door. I unlocked and turned the knob. Ethan's brows were knitted together in anger as he saw Kyle and the gun. He lifted his hands up. "Let her go Kyle. It's me you really want."

Kyle pulled me back with him. "Shut the door asshole." Ethan's eyes veered to Trooper as he barked and growled at Marco, thrashing his head back and forth against the wire noose wrapped around his neck.

"It's not you I want, you piece of shit biker trash!" Kyle leaned into me, inhaling against my cheek "Its Fiona I want. She belongs to me! And that dog belongs to me!"

It happened so fast. Ethan's eyes were full of flaming rage. He snarled and propelled himself toward us. Kyle aimed the gun at him and fired. I screamed as the bullet sliced the side of Ethan's shoulder. But it didn't stop him. He charged at Kyle grabbing his wrist, forcing him to aim the gun up and away. With a loud bang, the gun went off again, that bullet penetrating the ceiling. I bolted, out of Kyle's hold, and darted away from under his arm. Ethan slammed his fist into Kyle's jaw and grabbed him around the waist, lifting and slamming his back against the wall. The side table was shoved, and a lamp crashed onto the floor.

Marco lost his grip on the restraint bar as Trooper jerked back, snarling. "Fuck!" he cried out as he sprinted out the front door. Trooper darted out the door and ran after Marco, barking, the restraint loop still wrapped around his neck, the bar trailing behind him.

Ethan and Kyle brawled on the floor, as Kyle pounded a fist into Ethan's bloody shoulder. Ethan shouted in pain as Kyle punched his shoulder again. He twisted himself away from Ethan, aiming to run out the door. But Ethan was quick and grabbed a hold of Kyle's ankle, tripping him. He fell, crashing, and landing on his chest and the side of his face. Ethan was back on him again, turning him over and pounding his fists into his face.

Ethan knocked him out cold, but his fists pounding against Kyle's face. I rushed to him, grabbing his bicep "Ethan!

Stop!" He turned his eyes to mine, full of rage. I clung to him and cried.

Ethan rose himself off Kyle, and lifting me with him, wrapping his arms around me. "Fiona," he pulled me away from him, his eyes roaming down my body, "you ok? Did he hurt you?"

I shook my head vigorously. "No. I'm ok." I leaned back into him, smelling the copper scent of his blood and gun powder. The right shoulder of his flannel shirt was covered in wet blood. Trooper trotted back into the house, panting and dragging the restraint pole behind him. He sat on his haunches right next to Ethan's feet.

Gunner

Several county deputies were at Fiona's house five minutes after I dialed. They put Kyle in handcuffs, getting him in the back of one of their cars. He dropped the gun when I drove him against the wall, and that was bagged for evidence, along with the bullet that hit my shoulder and lodged in the wall. Paramedics came to work on my shoulder. Luckily the bullet just nicked it and didn't damage any muscle or bone. They put me in the back of an ambulance even through I argued against it. Fiona rode with me to the Stayford Hospital where they cleaned and stitched up the wound and looked her over to make sure she had no injuries.

Ratchet, Sam, Skully, and Tanya came to the hospital, along with Spider. They were relieved that both me and Fiona were ok, as Sam and Tanya huddled around Fiona, comforting her. She was white as a ghost, but her fear subsided because they were all there for us. Her girlfriend Destiny showed up later, crying and holding Fiona. I understood now when Fiona told me about Destiny having no filter as she yelled in the hallway at the hospital, calling Kyle everything from limp dick to motherfucking asshole. Spider didn't know her, but he stepped up telling her to pipe down and take it down a notch. She did, even though her eyes glared at Spider.

The hospital released us before sunrise giving me some meds to fight off any infection from my shoulder wound. Skully and Tanya gave us a ride back to Fiona's house, with Trooper greeting us with lots of excitement. I helped Fiona clean up things that got broken in the house from the scuffle between me and Kyle. He followed us to her bedroom but laid down on the floor at the foot of her bed. We both stripped and climbed into her bed together. I held her tight in my arms as her cheek rested on my chest, she clung to me tight and began to sob.

"I blacked out the moment I saw Kyle. With that gun. Holding you against him. I was going to kill him. Because I wouldn't be able to breathe again if something happened to you Fiona." Even at that moment, my cock was painfully hard.

Fiona swiftly climbed on top of me and straddled her soft warm thighs over my hips. She impaled herself completely with my hard cock and cried out as I became balls deep inside her. "I belong to you, Ethan. Only you."

I was just as quick and rolled Fiona underneath me. I growled, thrusting my hips hard, ramming into her even more, possessing her. I felt sharp pain in my wounded shoulder as her fingers gripped on as she cried out at my relentless claiming of her body. "Yes. Fiona!" I pulled out and thrusted roughly back into her again "You understand now. I own you."

Fiona was fast asleep after I claimed her mouth, and her delicious body over and over for a few hours. I couldn't help myself. She turned me into a lust filled animal, only wanting to make her mine. I climbed out of her bed, covering her up with her comforter and kissing her forehead. She didn't even open her eyes but sighed with a smile on her face. I got dressed, telling Trooper to get up on the bed and watch over her.

I got in my truck and headed over to the clubhouse to meet with up my Chaos brothers. Spider poured me a shot of whiskey when I arrived, throwing down a few with me. I was chomping at the bit to find out all he knew about that other fuck-wad, Marco.

And Spider never disappointed either. "This Marco dip shit. From what I could find out from my friends over at the County Sheriff's office, he's got a criminal record. Just the typical shit – drugs, possession of firearms, blah blah. That's why Kyle was at Fiona's. He wanted the dog back and Marco was there to help him. I've got a good hunch there's some illegal dog fighting going on somewhere in this county brother."

The whiskey shots felt good as it warmed my throat and chest going down. I gave Spider a hard pat on his shoulder "I can always count on you for the intel. Thanks brother. We'll find him."

Marco sat in a wooden chair, with his chin slumped to his chest, snoring. All my Chaos brothers contributed to the full bucket of piss that Rocky tossed onto the sleeping fuck. Marco's eyes opened as he sputtered and spitted. He woke up to feel his arms bound behind his back to the chair. He shook his head a few times, then focused his eyes on me as Rocky dropped the empty bucket of piss.

Marco's brain finally registered. "What the fuck!" He didn't recognize Rocky, but he recognized me, and his eyes grew wide. He struggled against the rope that constricted him to the chair.

We had him in empty lot behind the Vibe. My Chaos brothers were standing alongside me, Ratchet, Spider, Skully, Magnet and Wez. Fiona's friend, Destiny, had done us a favor. She spotted Marco at a local bar a week later. She flirted with him and slipped something into his drink. And we took it from there.

I had Trooper tethered to a chain leash attached to his collar. I gripped the leather strap as it he pulled it taught. He growled as he bared his teeth bare, his crystal blue eyes locked on Marco.

"Fuck!" Marco shouted as I kept a tight hold on the leash. "It was Kyle's fucking brilliant idea, not mine! Keep that dog away from me!"

I smiled and gave a bit of slack on the leash. "Me and my brothers here want to watch him chew your fuckin balls off. But that would be letting you off way too easy. You'll get what you deserve motherfucker. It'll be in court, unless your dog fighting business partners get to you first."

Chaos Kings turned Marco over to the county's sheriff's department, drenched in Chaos piss. Bail was set for both Kyle and Marco to stand trial in early spring. Marco was now a marked man by the underground dog fighting syndicate. He was shitting his pants in fear for his life, because when he walked out of the county jail, he would be dead within a few weeks. Kyle was royally fucked as well. He could've written his own sad country song, about how he lost his wife, his career, and his house in that upscale neighborhood outside of Washington, DC.

Fiona

Ethan called me his ole lady and spent most of his evenings with me and Trooper at my house. He couldn't keep his hands off me, ravishing me anytime and anywhere he found the opportunity: in my bed, on the couch, in the shower, and even on my kitchen counter. The chilly fall weather was time spent with the Chaos Kings at their clubhouse too. My friendships with the women of the Chaos Coven grew stronger as they welcomed me with warm and open hearts. It was the first time I felt I belonged and didn't feel judged for what I did for a living. I was glowing with happiness from the inside.

The more Ethan told me about his tribe, The Chaos Kings, he opened my eyes to his view of the biker sub-culture. That not all men who ride a motorcycle and wear vests and patches were outlaws. The men in his club respected their women and were protective in a very primitive way. The Chaos Kings supported their community by hosting charity poker runs and volunteered to help with other functions. But the most important thing that Ethan showed me was that it's not a patch that signifies who you are. It's the things you do and how you treat others and live your own life that signifies the kind of man or woman you are. You get back what you hand out, and that Karma is part of our chaotic world.

    Ethan sat and mingled with his Chaos brothers at the bar in The Vibe. They were all there to thank Markus for giving both me and Destiny jobs. The Chaos Kings presence at the club was also meant to show the county that The Vibe was a legitimate gentleman's club. Destiny filled me in on a bit more about Markus. In the past, he did make his money dealing in prostitution and drugs and was in prison for a few years. But he cleaned up his act as he served his sentence and started all over again and went legitimate. There was no organized crime involvement with The Vibe and Markus worked with local law enforcement to keep his business safe.

    I was in the dressing room, chatting with the other dancers, as Destiny just got off the stage, hurrying through the door, wiping sweat off her breasts and neck. "Day-um Cherri! I didn't know that oh- so-fine Chaos King was here tonight! I'd like to find out if *he's* hung like a horse!"

    I stood in front of the mirror making sure my barely-there little dress was in place before my turn on stage. I looked at Destiny, shaking my head. "Such things you say my darling Destiny." I guess nothing she said shocked me anymore. "He's the VP, remember?"

"Oh I remember him from the hospital alright! You think he'd be up to buying me a drink?"

Knowing Destiny now for a few years, and she never acted tongue tied around men before. So, seeing the gleam in her eyes when she spoke about Spider, was adorable. "I'm sure he would. After all, you did help us all out by getting Marco."

"Well that was the *least* I could do! Marco had it coming. So, did Kyle. I hope their dicks rot and fall off. "

Ethan's eyes pivoted to me as he sat at the bar with Ratchet and Spider. Coming toward him with Destiny I could see that he had a relaxed expression, and the side of his mouth lifted as we approached, arm in arm. Spider turned around, and his eyes met Destiny's instantly. "Is it ok for Destiny to sit with you while I go up on stage next?"

Spider's handsome grin lit up his face as he patted the empty barstool beside him. "Hop on up here Destiny. I'll buy a drink."

Destiny batted her eyes at him, and climbed onto the barstool, wigging a bit, arching her back out so that Spider could admire her cleavage in a low cut shimmering tank top.

I moved to stand in between Ethan's legs. He wrapped his sturdy, robust arms around me, and nuzzled his scruffy beard against to my cheek. "You got any baby bibs behind the bar Darlin? I'm going to have to put one on Spider here in a few minutes."

I giggled. "She wants to find out if Spider is well endowed."

Ethan leaned back, his brows lifting in surprise at what I just said. "So you women DO talk just as dirty as us men, huh?"

I winked. "We sure do, my biker man. And I don't blush anymore about it either."

Ethan smacked my ass hard, making me squeal. "Such a naughty girl…" He growled low. "Now go up there and dance for me darlin. Show all these men in here that rosy mark I just left on that nice hot ass of yours."

My tongue darted out and drew a wet path across his lower lip. I scooted out of his grasp and sashayed onto the stage. I danced to the haunting theme song from the show "True Blood". The twangy guitar sound came through the speakers in beat with Jace Everett's deep sultry voice, as I performed hip swivels, hook spins, fireman spins and carousel slides around the silver pole.

Gunner

I nudged Spider next to me, interrupting his conversation with Destiny, "There he is." I nodded my head toward the man, sitting alone at a table in the corner, wearing a hoodie. He followed the rules of the club and pulled the hood back once he sat down. I couldn't make out his age, because his jaw was covered with a full grown beard and his hair was shaggy and messy, down to his shoulders.

Spider spotted him too and turned back to me. "Yeah. I see him. Same dude, huh?"

"Yeah." I knocked back another shot of whiskey, watching the man as he watched Fiona on stage. I knew Fiona was safe at the Vibe, but I'd seen this man there before, several times. He always came alone and left after Fiona danced. Just like I used to do at the Cheetah.

Wads of bills clung to Fiona's hips and ass like a belt, strapped under her thong, as she sashayed off the stage. She headed down the hall to the dressing room, and the next second I was off my bar stool, when the man in the hoodie got up from his chair, looked toward me first, and then turned to follow Fiona.

He was only a few feet from her, as I gripped his shoulder, slamming his back against the wall. He reached up, grabbing my cut and shoved me back toward the other side of the hallway. He knocked my back against the wall and I didn't anticipate that he could be as strong as I was, because my head was full of rage again, just as it was with Kyle. I swung at him, and my knuckles connected with his jaw. His fists came off my cut, as he staggered back.

The sound of Fiona's cry stopped both of us. Her eyes were wide with shock. The man reached up and wiped blood from the corner of his mouth with his knuckles. He turned to Fiona and pulled his hood back.

She recognized him. She knew him. She rushed to him and threw her arms around his shoulders. "Seth!"

He wrapped his arms around Fiona, burying his face into her hair "It's me Fiona." She began to cry and so did Seth.

With my back against the wall, I leaned over to steady my breathing and the pounding in my chest. At that moment, watching them in each other's arms reminded me of my sister Gabby. And that I missed her. I raked a hand through my hair, shaking my head and turned away.

.

"Ethan, wait!" I looked back at Fiona, to see tears streaking down the sides of her flushed cheeks.

I reached up, and brushed her wet cheek with my calloused thumb. "Go talk to him Fiona. I'll be right here."

She smiled as I left her with Seth and went back to the bar. I let Spider know the man was her brother.

Spider chuckled, shaking his head. "You're always thinkin with your fists Gunner. You throw a punch, then ask questions later!"

Seth drove his car and followed us back Fiona's house later that night. I parked my truck in front of her house, and leaned over to her, brushing my lips across hers. "You need some time alone with your bother. To catch up. "

I got out of my truck, walking around to Fiona's side, but Seth was already there, his hands shoved in his pockets. That's when I got a better look at him under the street light in front of her house. Seth had Fiona's eyes, the same shade of pale blue. He looked like just turned twenty-one, even with man's full grown beard. His blond hair was shaggy, down past his shoulders. I couldn't make out his build because of the oversized hoodie he wore that was zipped up, but he matched me in height and strength.

I reached out my hand to him. "Sorry about that man." Looking at the corner of his mouth, and the blood dried.

He looked down and shook it. "It's nothin. I'm used to it."

I let him open the truck door for Fiona. I gave her another kiss, got back in my truck and drove home, leaving brother and sister together for the first time in years that night.

Fiona

That night both of us talked cried and held each other. Seth told me things and I knew he was victimized by our father too. But there was only so much Seth would tell me, and I didn't press him. He wanted to keep to himself and buried deep.

After I had left, things just got worse. Seth was a few years younger than me, but I could see it in his eyes what he had seen and what he had felt. There was so much pain. He always had a boyish face, with feminine angles to it. His blond was unkept and had grown past his shoulders. He had a full beard that made him look even older than he was.

"I hated him. I hated everyone. There was nothing I could do but hitch it out of town. I've done things Fiona. Things I had to do, just to survive on the streets. I made it up north to New York. I did some underground fighting to make money, so I could eat, or have a bed to sleep in.   I've even shacked up with men! Men who gave me a bed to sleep in, and food, and nice clothes." His voice was deeper than I remembered, and sad.

"I called back home to mother when I could. And she finally left our dear ole dad. She moved in with Aunt Cheryl.

Father breathed to keep his black hear pumping. I don't even think he had a soul, spitting out all those fucking bible verses to us! Mother told me he drank more and more and then he had a stroke, that landed him a nursing home. Now he's lying in a bed full of his own shit and piss. People are tending to his miserable ass every day as he still breaths. And he's already dead."

"I did what I could to protect you and mother, Fiona." Seth's head dropped down, his hands combing through his shaggy hair.

I was on my knees at his feet, and reached up, wrapping my arms around him. "I know Seth. But you were just a child. And so was I. Children are to be loved and cherished and protected by their parents." I pulled his hands away, so I could look into his eyes. "Seth, don't blame yourself. Don't blame others. Its not your fault. The only one to blame is him. And mother is safe now. I'm safe now. And you are here. With me."

Seth's eyes were still sad, but his mouth lifted with a hint of a smile. He leaned down and scooped me up in his arms. Arms that were more muscular than I remembered. He looked down at me, that sad smile still there. "You don't need me around to be safe, sis. Looks like your biker boyfriend has it all covered."

My biker boyfriend. I flushed and felt so warm and happy inside. "Yes, Ethan. He understands me. I'm in love with him. He cherishes me. Protects me. He looks at me as if I'm the most beautiful woman he's ever seen. He's a member of the Chaos Kings MC. They call him Gunner. He served in the Army and is a war veteran. His club is legitimate. They are a family all their own, like a tribe. They have all made me feel welcome and its where I belong. I belong with Ethan."

"Good. Ethan's strong right hook to my jaw just proved it to me!" He chuckled, making me laugh. "It's really good to see you smile sis. You look happy."

"I am Seth. And the icing on top of all my happiness is having my brother back in my life too."

Within a month, Seth felt more at ease and grounded. Ethan made him feel welcome too. He introduced Seth to his club brothers, and Wez gave him a job working at his tattoo shop, Mad Ink, talking to new clients, setting up appointments and helping around the shop. Tanya was so kind and did a total makeover on Seth. She cut his hair and trimmed up his beard. And I saw the young boy I remembered, who had to be a man to protect his family at such a youthful age. His face was more masculine, with an angular jaw and his bright blue eyes appeared wiser.

He didn't talk much, but he never really did even when he was young. He was much more introverted than me and like to be alone most of the time. Trooper warmed up to Seth and followed along beside him like he used to do with me. And I didn't pry to ask him more about his life before he showed up at the Cheetah. I just hoped he would be willing to share his experiences with me someday when and if he was ever ready.

We invited Seth to the clubhouse a few times and he seemed to a have a connection with Skully. Tanya had told me a little about Skully's childhood as an orphan, living in foster homes all through his childhood until he was eighteen. And how he had done some things in his past that he was not proud of but wanted to be the best man he could be for her and for his son, little Jake, who looked just like him. Maybe Skully could sense this from Seth, that they both did what they needed to survive. And to do it alone.

It was a very chilly November night as Ethan drove me home from our date at the movies. It was nice to have a date night, just us two, making out in the theater even before the movie began. Ethan's warm hand glided up under my sweater as we kissed. He tugged my bra cup down, rolling my hard nipple between his thumb and forefinger. I sucked in a breath as he whispered in my ear as the beginning credits to the movie appeared on the screen. "I like feeling you up at the movies, my naughty little vixen."

I giggled. We felt like two horny teenagers, as Ethan left me wet and wanting him for two hours as I endured watching the movie. But he suffered too, as he shifted in his seat with a raging hard on.

Ethan's truck beamed its headlights through the dusting of snowflakes as he drove me to his house. And he drove a little above the speed limit, wanting to get me back to his place so we could finish what we both started in the theater.

He looked over at me, with hunger in his eyes and a devilish grin. "Once I get you back to my place, I'm gonna to wear that sexy-as-fuck body of yours." I batted my eyes at him, trying to look innocent. But his eyes turned back to the road and his smile faded. "I've been thinkin lately darlin. About how I'm always taking you back to my place."

My heart was floating above the clouds for months now, but at that very moment, my heart sank. "Are you bored with me?"

His eyes pivoted back to me. "God no Fiona! I'm never bored with you! Sometimes I wish I could keep you in my bed for days! How about you move into my place? I know it's not much, but Ratchet's basement would be enough for the both us. Think about it, sleeping on your couch is probably getting kind of old for Seth anyway."

My chest flushed back up with warmth, and my eyes began to swell with tears. Of happiness. He reached over, splaying his warm hand on my thigh. His brows lifted. "You like that idea don't you darlin."

My hand covered his. "Yes Ethan. I do."

Gunner

Fiona moved in a week later. We had Seth over and shared Thanksgiving dinner with Ratchet and Sam. Me, and Seth sat up in Ratchets living room, watching football and drinkin beers, while Sam and Fiona did their female bonding in the kitchen, fluttering around like little birds. They did a fantastic job cooking the turkey and all the fixings. We had a fun time, laughing. Just being around people I cared about made me remember my family and how I grew up. I had good memories of both my dad and mom, and my younger sister, Gabby, even though she was a bit of a tomboy as a kid. Then one day, she just blossomed into a pretty teenager, with me fighting off the boys in high school, before I enlisted in the Army.

I could only imagine what it was like for both Fiona and Seth growing up, with a cruel and hateful drunk monster for a father and a mother who couldn't protect them. Seth didn't say much, but he was a good brother to Fiona, only wanting to protect her like I did with Gabby. Whatever he had to do to survive on the streets alone and come back to Fiona alive, was a good thing.

A few nights later, Chaos got together to pound down some beers and shots at the clubhouse. Everyone brought leftovers from Thanksgiving dinners to finish off, my brothers and the coven in jovial holiday moods. I just downed a shot of whiskey as Ratchet came in with Sam. She rushed over to Fiona standing by the jukebox with Tanya, whispering in their ears. Before Ratchet lumbered over to me sitting the bar, he smacked Sam on her ass, making her jump and yelp. Ratchet cracked out a chuckle as Sam turned a shade of pink and the girls giggled.

"Pour me one of those brother," Ratchet grumbled, with a big grin on his face.

I poured him a shot and another for myself, handing him his. "What was THAT all about?"

Ratchet lit a smoke, "What?" turning toward the women. "Oh. That. It's not MY fault my ole lady is blushing. That's Fiona's fault."

"And how is it Fiona's fault? *You're* the one that smacked Sam on the ass. And hard enough, everyone in the clubhouse heard it, asshole."

"Cuz Sam surprised me with a lap dance last night. And it was the hottest fuckin lap dance I ever got! But I might have given it back to her a little much though. She's walking all funny again. So that's why it's Fiona's fault brother. She's taught my ole lady some sexy dance moves!"

I chuckled. So *that* was what Fiona and Sam were chirping in each other's ears about that night Fiona danced on the pool table. And I fucked on it too.

Ratchet raised his shot glass to me. "She's been ridden hard."

I knocked mine against his. "And put away wet." We threw back the whiskey at the same time and slammed the glasses back on the bar.

"She amazes me Gunner. After all the fucked up shit she's been through, she's come out of her shell and shows me just how fuckin beautiful she is."

"Yeah Ratchet. She's a bad-ass little woman."

I remembered Ratchet talking to me not too long ago, about coming out of my shell, right there at the clubhouse bar. Everything was all bottled up inside me when I came back from the war, out of the Army, and back to civilian life. I struggled with rage, and violent tendencies ever since. Then I found Fiona. The red haired vixen whose soft touch, and sweet velvety voice, calmed the pounding headaches. I wanted her the moment I saw her dancing around that pole at the Cheetah. Even possessive instincts even kicked in around my brothers that night at Skully's patch in party.

I started to think about my family back home in Maryland again too, and realized I missed them. A lot. I pulled my phone out, and headed out to the parking lot, telling Ratchet, "Gonna make a phone call. I'll be back."

I pushed the button on the screen on my phone that said "Home". It rang a few times.

"Ethan?" Gabby answered.

"Yeah Gabby. It's Ethan. Happy Thanksgiving."

I heard a huffy breath on her end. "You're a few days late. You *should* have come over. Mom and Dad had all the family here for Thanksgiving dinner. "

"Sorry sis. I'll make it up to everyone. I'll come by during the Christmas holiday."

There was silence for a few seconds. "That'd be really nice Ethan." I heard her sniffle. "Mom and Dad miss you so much. So do I."

"Yeah. I miss them too."

"What about me? You're only fucking sister!"

"Damit Gabby! I miss you too."

Some things never changed. Like our big brother, little sister bickering. "And I want you to meet my ole lady. I mean, girlfriend." *Girlfriend?*

"I want to meet her too. What's her name?"

"Fiona. She's gorgeous and amazing."

"Well she *better* be amazing if she's dating *my* big brother!"

I chuckled. "She's got a brother too. His name is Seth and I'll bring him over with us. Got it?"

"Got it. Are you going to give Mom and Dad a call too?"

"Sure. I'll give them a call tonight. I'll see you soon sis."

"Ok Ethan. I love you!"

"I Love you too Gabby."

Epilogue

I draped my forearm over my eyes to block the muted sunlight coming through the bedroom window. Cradled in the crook of my other arm was Fiona. Her soft naked body pressed alongside mine. My cock started to get hard, like it always did when I was next to her.

Gypsy hopped onto my bed again last night, curled up, sleeping at our feet over the covers. The sound of four paws thumping came from the stairs that lead down to the basement. Trooper's muzzle appeared from the door as he pushed it open. Gypsy was suddenly up on all fours, her claws out, her hackles raised, looking like a fur-ball that just exploded. She hissed at Trooper. He barked back. She hissed again and leaped off the bed, bounding over Trooper and bolted out the door. I chuckled, shaking my head.

They woke up Fiona. I looked at her, cradled next to me. She nuzzled her cheek against my nipple and yawned. She opened her eyes and smile up at me, her bright blue eyes so captivating. My hand squeezed her naked soft ass, and she flinched and yelped.

"So sorry darlin…" I just remembered why her ass cheek was a bit sore. I gave Fiona her Christmas gift last night.

Actually, Wez gave her my gift – on her left ass cheek. As she laid on the bench at his parlor, Wez marked her gorgeous derrière with his tattoo gun – a red heart, surrounded by tribal designs. And inside the heart were the words, "Property of Gunner.". Ever since she moved in, she insisted every day that she wanted this. So, I gave it to her. Just picturing Fiona dancing on the pole at The Vibe, showing everyone that she belonged to me made my heart skip a beat.

Fiona moaned. "You were in my dreams. And now I'm wet for you." Her sleepy voice was music to my ears. I was ready to plunge my hard dick deep up inside her.

But that would have to wait until later. I titled her chin up and looked into her eyes. "You're gonna stay wet for me all day darlin. Seth's already here with Trooper. We have a full day."

It was Christmas morning, and I looked forward looking forward to seeing my family again and couldn't wait to introduce Fiona and Seth to them. I brushed my thumb across her bottom lip. "You're not nervous anymore, are you? About meeting my family?" She worried that they wouldn't like her. Or Seth.

"From the things you've told me about them, and how much you love them, No. I'm not worried anymore."

"Good. My sister Gabby can be a bit spunky at times, like your friend Destiny. But I already know she's gonna love you."

So, for the first time, in a long time, I felt grounded. Yeah, I still battled the darkness and rage at times, but I didn't battle with myself anymore. I wanted to reach out to everyone that I loved and show them love back.

THE END

About Linny Lawless

Linny grew up in Northern Virginia, right outside Washington DC, and has a professional career in sales operations for over 20 years. She's also spent 13 years riding with her husband on the back of a Harley! Linny loves the feeling of freedom, wildness, and rebellion that comes with it. The biker community can be tribal and primal at times.

Linny has also been a huge book worm since she was a young teen. She reads different genres of books, but the one Linny loves the most is Romance! She self-published her debut novel, "Salvation in Chaos" in January of 2018. Her stories are about scruffy, sexy alpha bikers who belong to a tribe, their club, and the women they fall in love with. They live in a world full of chaos, not unlike reality. But within that chaotic world, they live their lives the best way they can and discover true love.

Books by Linny Lawless

"Salvation in CHAOS"

Amazon US: http://a.co/9kmkT6b
Amazon UK: http://amzn.eu/6WBQECT
Amazon CA: http://a.co/d6OLuWa

Available on other Platforms
https://www.books2read.com/u/b5rZa6

"Deep in CHAOS"

Amazon:
https://www.amazon.com/dp/B07BJ83QT9

Available on other Platforms
https://www.books2read.com/u/bzPjwG

"Summer Heat Anthology"
https://www.amazon.com/dp/B07D4RCMVX

Linny Lawless Social Media Links

Facebook page: https://www.facebook.com/Linnylawlessromance/
Street Team: https://www.facebook.com/groups/1481551685255429/
Website: https://linnylawless.com/
Instagram: https://www.instagram.com/linnylawless/
Goodreads: https://www.goodreads.com/user/show/73729078-linny-lawless
BookBub: https://www.bookbub.com/authors/linny-lawless

Newsletter Sign Up

https://mailchi.mp/772f49e20225/linnylawlessnewsletter

Made in the USA
Middletown, DE
14 April 2019